She tried to ...
came out.

Brody stood in the doorway looking equally shocked to see her after so long. His green eyes seemed glued to her. His six-foot-plus frame filled the space. He hadn't shaved. Mussed brown hair that had been cut shorter when she'd been with him had sprouted waves, and a few curls brushed his neck behind his ears. His jaw was strong, but tense. His lips, as tempting as ever.

Then his face broke into a welcoming smile, his eyes warming from surprise to pleasure. Hannah didn't have a chance to move away as he encompassed her in a bear hug. Soon, those delectable lips were all over hers.

His beard scratched her a little, but Hannah was so blindsided by the unexpected embrace that she held on for dear life, her internal temperature skyrocketing as Brody's tongue parted her lips and sought out hers.

Stop this, her brain said.

Just one more minute, her very happy heart argued. It was like getting a charge from a lightning bolt.

She couldn't help but smile into his kiss. This was Brody.

He was never what she expected. But it was always good...

Dear Reader,

If you have read *I'll Be Yours for Christmas* (and if you haven't, go get it right now!), you met racing champion Brody Palmer and accountant Hannah Morgan in the subplot of that book. When I sent these two off on a wild month in Daytona, I knew there was more to the story—what happened after that month? So *Rock Solid* came to be. Though not easily; these characters made sure I found the right story for them.

Writers talk about their characters making decisions about the book, and I'd never experienced that, exactly...until I wrote Hannah and Brody. When Brody made his big plot move in the middle of the book, *I* didn't even see it coming, let alone poor Hannah. He really is a wild man, and he surprised us both with his daring ways. Watching him grow from a playboy into the solid man that Hannah loves was an adventure in itself.

If you want to chat about *Rock Solid*, or any of my Harlequin Blaze books, you can find me on Twitter or Facebook most days, and I'd love to hear from you.

Samantha Hunter

Samantha Hunter

—

Rock Solid

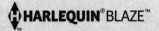

HARLEQUIN® BLAZE™

Recycling programs
for this product may
not exist in your area.

ISBN-13: 978-0-373-79837-7

Rock Solid

Copyright © 2015 by Samantha Hunter

Printed in U.S.A.

Samantha Hunter lives in Syracuse, New York, where she writes full-time for Harlequin. When she's not plotting her next story, Sam likes to work in her garden, quilt, cook, read and spend time with her husband and their dogs. Most days you can find Sam chatting on the Harlequin Blaze boards at Harlequin.com, or you can check out what's new, enter contests or drop her a note at her website, samanthahunter.com.

Books by Samantha Hunter

HARLEQUIN BLAZE

Talking in Your Sleep...
Hard to Resist
Caught in the Act
Make Your Move
I'll Be Yours for Christmas
Mine Until Morning
Straight to the Heart
Yours for the Night
Hers for the Holidays
His Kind of Trouble
Unforgettable
Unexpected Temptation
"Holiday Rush" in *Wild Holiday Nights*

Visit the Author Profile page at Harlequin.com for more titles

Thank you to Brandi H, who was named in this book in gratitude for her generous donation to the 2013 Brenda Novak Auction.

Many friends saw me through a long winter when the writing was difficult, most specifically the ladies at Chocolate Box Writers (chocolateboxwriters.com) who fielded many emails from me with grace, patience and a multitude of helpful suggestions. You are all amazing. Lucky me.

Brilliant writers Anne Calhoun and Serena Bell, who read the manuscript at various stages, brainstormed and also helped me figure out what wasn't working and what was—amid their own very busy schedules. So many hugs to you.

Cari Quinn offered companionship and a lot of laughs and motivation during working lunches at Panera. She also thinks it's funny when I talk back to my book—out loud.

And always, for Mike—for everything you do, thank you is never enough.

Prologue

"I'M NOT RETIRING," Brody said definitively. "You asked me to think about it, and I thought about it. The answer is no."

Jud Harris, the lead publicist and marketing liaison for the corporate sponsor who had made his racing possible for the past five years, leaned in.

"Brody, I'm afraid it's not optional at this point. After that fiasco at the club, it was all I could do to talk the heads of the company into keeping you on at all. You need to play ball and seriously clean up your act."

Play ball. Yeah, right. Brody curled his fists under the table, trying to control his anger as he kept his voice level.

"I've got a pretty healthy bank account, Jud. I can finance my own car and team."

It would probably take everything he had, but he could manage it for a year or two, until he could get another sponsor.

If you can get another sponsor, a traitorous doubt in his brain taunted.

"C'mon, Brody, we drop you, it looks bad. Your

other, smaller sponsors would follow. We've put up with a lot over the years, but now we need to do damage control. We're just asking you to lie low for a while. Stay out of trouble and the gossip pages."

Brody bit out a curse, knowing Jud was right. Sponsorship was about more than money, as well—sponsors were a part of the team's image and a vote of confidence. They also created community—people who worked for or were customers of that sponsor supported the car and the team.

"I told you why I was there—"

"It doesn't matter what really happened. It matters how it showed up in the news."

Brody stood, needing to get some distance before he really lost his temper. He knew what Jud said was true, and that was what was eating at him.

He'd been in the wrong place at the wrong time, helping a friend—a married friend—who'd called from a notorious kink club, too drunk to drive. Reporters who hung around those places waiting for a story revealed Brody coming out of the club at three in the morning.

He was judged in the eyes of the media, and caught in a situation where he couldn't reveal his real reason for being there. Not publicly. He didn't care as much about protecting his friend, who shouldn't have been there in the first place, as he did the three kids the guy had at home. They didn't need to see their father's picture on the news. Not like that.

So Brody let the public think what they wanted.

The playboy image he'd earned over the years meant it would be passed off as one more chapter in the story of wild Brody Palmer.

Jud took his silence as possible receptivity and continued to press.

"Besides, it's not actual retirement, we'll just play it that way to the press. It will amp up interest. Your fans love you. They'll miss you and want you back. Then you return, we build it up and it's a big deal. It's been done before, in a lot of sports."

"And what am I supposed to do in the meantime?"

"You settle down. Maybe find a nice girl and get married…or at least engaged. You can always break it off later. We'll stage your comeback, you'll come back the season after next, bigger than ever. The game is changing, Brody. People are more family oriented these days. Your lifestyle… Well, we have to protect the brand. *Our* brand," Jud said firmly.

Brody thought his head would explode as Jud kept talking. He'd always enjoyed himself—in the car, he was all business, but in his life, he did what he wanted. He made his own rules. Until now.

Racing was his life. Driving was like breathing to him. The idea of losing it… He couldn't let that happen.

If the sponsor bailed, it would affect the whole team. This wasn't only about him. Other livelihoods, reputations and futures were on the line, as well. They might be able to move to other work, but not right away. And not all of them.

"You'll keep paying the team salaries?" Brody interrupted.

"Absolutely. We'll say it's part of your retirement deal that they are paid out for the season, but they can't know the truth. No one can. If this gets out, it would be a mess for everyone. Understand? Then the deal's off, period."

Brody nodded.

"Trust me," Jud said. "This will work. But you need to do your part and really change your behavior. Ten years ago, you could get away with this stuff, but people are less willing to accept it now."

Yeah, he understood. He had to stop racing for a year and lie to everyone he knew. Brody understood just fine. It didn't sit well. There were some lines he didn't cross: he didn't sleep with married women, he never broke a promise and he didn't lie. He had enough other vices to keep him in the news, but those were three he'd always held true, until now.

Every bone in his body rejected the idea, but he had to think of his team and his future. It was only one season, and then he would come back, stronger than ever.

He'd make sure of it.

"Fine. Draw up the paperwork."

Brody walked out the door before he even heard Jud's reply, but when he made his way out of the office building in downtown Manhattan, he stood on the sidewalk, feeling lost. Blending himself into the crowd on the street, he couldn't help but wonder: What the heck was he going to do with himself for the next year?

1

Hannah Morgan sat alone in a dimly lit Atlanta bar, a plate of ribs sitting untouched to her left, a bottle of beer to her right, and her laptop opened directly in front of her. Growling in frustration at the laptop, she pushed it away to grab the ribs and dig in.

Quitting her accounting job had seemed like the right thing to do two months ago, but now she was having serious doubts. At the time, she'd been passed over for yet another promotion and had finally asked her boss why she was always being rejected for promotions at the firm she'd always given her best to.

You play it too safe to handle the bigger clients, Hannah, her boss had told her. *They need someone who can think outside the box, find creative solutions.*

Too safe?

She hadn't been aware that being sensible or responsible was a bad thing in financial management, she fumed for the thousandth time as she tore into a rib.

Well, she'd shown them. She'd quit. That was hardly playing it safe, right? Neither was taking off around the country to explore her options and try to start a new career. Now she was operating completely outside the box.

Take that, she grumped as she licked the spicy, smoky sauce from her fingers and then took another from the plate. She'd missed lunch while working on her photo blog, *Hannah's Great Adventure*, which so far hadn't been very adventurous at all.

It wasn't that she hadn't tried, but adventure and risk taking had never come naturally to her.

She eyed the few comments she did have on her blog.

Nice.

Pretty.

Then there was the one that asked if she had any pictures of herself, and when would she come to his town?

Ugh. That was not the kind of adventure she was looking for.

Unfortunately, though she was active on social media and always posting on her blog, traffic was low. But she was still new at this, right? It would take time to establish and make a name for herself.

Sighing, she pushed the plate aside and bolstered her resolve as she pulled the laptop back, front and center. At least she could finish an assignment for the online writing course she was taking. Years as an accountant had left her writing skills somewhat rusty.

Just as her concentration took hold, someone slid into the seat opposite her.

"You don't like the ribs?"

A gorgeous guy, complete with a sexy Southern

accent and a wicked smile, looked at her inquiringly, making her mind stutter for a moment.

"Um, no, they're wonderful," she replied, and then saw the shirt he was wearing had the name of the bar stamped over one well-defined pectoral muscle.

"Well, I thought I should check, as you pushed the plate away. I have to make sure customers are satisfied, especially the pretty ones," he said with a sexy wink, making her laugh.

He was flat-out gorgeous and charming to boot. And flirting with *her.* Suddenly her blog wasn't all that interesting.

"Thanks," she said, cringing inwardly as she wished she was a better flirt.

"My name's Jarvis," he said, holding his hand out. "You work nearby? Or are you a student at the university?" He looked at the laptop inquiringly.

She took his hand, finding his grasp pleasant and warm, strong but not smothering. Hannah let him hold on for another second or two, and liked the gentle squeeze he offered at the end.

"Neither. I'm a photojournalist. Well, I want to be one. It was something I wanted to do in college, but never followed through on. So I'm taking a year to travel the country to explore, to…blog. Try to develop, you know, a focus…or something," she said, realizing she was babbling and stopping before she made a real fool of herself. This guy wasn't really interested in her life history, she was sure.

"So you're only passing through?" Jarvis asked with even more pronounced interest this time. Clearly not looking for commitment, which was fine with her.

Hannah was about to respond when a sportscast

from one of the televisions positioned all around the bar caught her eye, stealing her attention away from her companion.

Brody.

Supersize on the screen, the stock-car champion's image still made her catch her breath. Well, former racing champion. It seemed as though there was always something around reminding her of him. A magazine cover, a news item or a fan wearing his number on a T-shirt or on a sticker on their car, even after his retirement six months ago.

She couldn't hear the story, but the picture they showed was from a year before, shortly after she'd parted ways with him. The headline noted five drivers who had recently left the track.

"You're into racing?" Jarvis asked, watching her watch Brody.

Hannah tore her gaze from the screen.

"Oh, no, not so much. I… He's a, um…a friend. But we haven't seen each other in a while."

"You keep interesting company."

Once. Once, she'd kept company for a wild month with Brody Palmer, and it was one of the best experiences of her life. Her only true adventure, ever.

She smiled at Jarvis, trying to get Brody out of her mind.

Hannah didn't have a whole lot of experience picking up men in bars, or letting them pick her up—but things were different now. Or at least, she wanted them to be.

She focused on Jarvis. He was real, and right here in front of her. Not an image on TV or a memory from the past. Maybe the sexy bartender was exactly what she needed in order to make some new, adventurous memories.

"I planned to leave tomorrow, but I'm flexible," she said, proud of her own flirtatious innuendo, taking a sip of her beer and peeking at him over the top of her glass.

Fifteen minutes later, they were kissing in his office.

It turned out Jarvis owned the bar, which was an added bonus, since he had a very nice office with a delicious leather couch and a large desk. Hannah had a feeling they might make use of both. Right now, he was wrapped around her with his warm, strong hands finding their way up to her bra strap.

Jarvis moved fast, and Hannah let him, trying to enjoy what this hot guy was doing to her and not letting the image of Brody's face on the TV screen—and the memories of his kiss, and his touch—ruin her fun.

But it was too late.

All she could think of was Brody. What was he doing since he retired? She'd considered contacting him, but it didn't seem wise.

As Jarvis was trailing his lips lower, her mind wandered.

Maybe Brody would like to see an old friend? Maybe…he could help her out? Be her first real, exciting story for her blog?

Why not? She was trying to write about something *exciting*—and the most exciting person she'd ever known was only about eight hours away.

Would he see her? Would he talk to her?

What if he said no?

"Hannah?" Jarvis's sexy voice broke through her thoughts.

He pulled back and looked at her questioningly, aware she had gone elsewhere, at least in her head. She backed away.

"I'm so sorry, I shouldn't have done this. We have to stop."

"What?" He seemed more disconcerted than angry, but Hannah couldn't go through with this. "Did I do something—"

"No, I promise, it's totally me. I'm too distracted. It's not your fault at all, I just… I have to go."

Jarvis's arms loosened and she apologized again, barely taking in his dazed look as she pictured meeting up with Brody. If she could take some pictures of him for her blog, that would put her on the map. He *was* retired. What was he up to? *That* was a blog she could write that would get some attention.

If he would agree. And why wouldn't he? They'd parted on good terms, and they were friends, right? If she wanted to make this work, she had to be bold.

Hannah tugged her clothes straight before she went out into the kitchen and then the bar, convincing herself that this was the right thing to do, and that Brody would want to see her again, as much as she wanted to see him.

BRODY JERKED AWAKE, suddenly alert as he peered around his room. Sunlight peeked through a crack in the curtains, making him squint as he checked the clock. It was just past nine. He didn't even recall when he'd gone to bed, though it had been late. The days all seemed to slide by recently, one blurring into the other. He peered at the half-empty bottle of Scotch on the dresser, and the glass by his bed.

That reminded him that his shoulder had been hurting like hell last night, and the alcohol was better than the pain pills the doctor prescribed. Well, somewhat anyway.

His shoulder was dislocated and sprained when his horse had thrown him. Luckily, nothing was broken.

Some luck.

If he'd been driving his stock car instead of riding Zip—the Thoroughbred colt he'd adopted from a rescue organization—none of this would have happened.

Racing might be dangerous, but the "quiet" life might kill him yet. Brody wasn't built for quiet.

At least he was getting back to where he could do some light work with the horses and drive. For several weeks after he'd been thrown, he thought he would go out of his mind with boredom. He was counting the days until his mandatory "retirement" was over; it couldn't happen soon enough.

Then he realized what had awakened him as the aroma of coffee drifted through the open door.

Someone *was* downstairs.

Was he with a woman last night? He didn't think he'd had so much to drink that he wouldn't remember. Though his sponsor had told him to behave, Brody wasn't much good at that, either. There had been a few women since he'd left the track. He had to have something to do.

He'd had contractors in for several months, renovating the old farm house from top to bottom, and he'd adopted some new horses, but apart from all that, sex was at least a temporary reprieve. Though, since that news item appeared saying he was looking to settle down he couldn't bring a girl home without her wanting to stay for good.

Now he tended to not go out. It was like being in prison. Walking to the window, he groaned when he saw a familiar car parked out front.

He must have drunk more than he usually did to have Jackie over. What a mess.

"Hey, sexy. Hungry?"

Jackie stood smiling inside his bedroom door, then she crossed the room to link her arms around his neck and kiss him before he could say anything. He turned his head, breaking the kiss and loosening her hold.

"Jackie, what are you doing here?"

She shrugged, pouting.

"I was in the neighborhood, so I thought I'd come over and surprise you with breakfast."

Brody brightened slightly. "So you just got here?"

"About an hour ago. I brought some muffins from the bakery you like, made coffee and I could put on some eggs, too. I thought you might like to work up more of an appetite first, though..."

He stepped away, putting some distance between them—he'd been trying to put a lot of distance between himself and Jackie. He'd explained it to her several times, but she was more persistent than he'd expected. She'd been a high school girlfriend and more recently...an impulse. A mistake.

He was thankful that at least he hadn't made it worse. She knew where he left his extra key, and had let herself in, obviously.

Grabbing some jeans from the chair, he pulled them on.

"Don't get dressed on my account."

Brody's only response was a withering look as he left the room. He could hear her heels on the hard-wood stairs close behind as he went to the front door.

"Jackie, I appreciate your making breakfast—"

"Then show me," she said, sidling up to him again and putting her arm through his.

Brody sighed, stepping back and putting her away from him, his patience threading thin. He wasn't interested.

"You need to go," he said bluntly. "We've already talked about this."

Her eyes turned diamond-chip hard as she set her hands on her hips, ready to argue. A knock at the door startled them both, and Brody almost groaned aloud. Who else was here this early in the morning? He was relatively private about where he lived, but still, fans and reporters seemed to find him more often than he liked.

"Hold on," he said, turning away from Jackie to see who it was.

When he swung open the door, though, he couldn't have been more shocked to see a familiar pair of blue eyes staring back at him.

2

HANNAH STARED AT BRODY, who wasn't on television this time, but standing only two feet in front of her.

She froze, unsure what to say, her bravado evaporating like the morning fog in the sun. Maybe this hadn't been such a good idea.

She'd driven all night, wanting to see him before she lost her nerve, but apparently she had lost it anyway. She'd gotten the address of his family's ranch from Abby, but he'd been hard to find, especially since she'd ended up navigating unmarked farm roads where her GPS had also lost its signal.

She was exhausted and hungry, but she was here. Part of her mind registered that it was one of the most flat-out beautiful properties she'd ever seen. The sprawling colonial farmhouse with its black shutters, enormous porch and pretty red door were classic. The brass race-car knocker on the door had let her know she was in exactly the right place. Lush green fields and trees surrounded the house, and several horses grazed in the pasture—it was like something from a postcard.

She tried to say his name, but no words came out.

Lifting her hand uselessly—to do what? Wave? Shake his hand?—she let it drop to her side again.

Thoughts scattered as she remembered how he used to look in the morning…naked, mussed head of hair, gleaming eyes…and sexy. Extremely sexy.

Brody's six-foot-plus frame filled the doorway. He hadn't shaved. Shaggy brown hair that had been cut shorter when she'd been with him had sprouted waves, and a few curls brushed his neck. His jaw was strong but tense. His lips as tempting as ever. He was shirtless, the top button on his jeans undone, as if he had only now gotten out of bed.

That brought back a wave of memories that nearly did send her running back to her car. What had she been thinking, coming here?

Then his face broke into a welcoming smile, his expression switching from surprise to pleasure. The next thing she knew, Brody encompassed her in a bear hug. Then his delectable mouth was all over hers, his bare torso flush against her.

Hannah forgot to breathe.

His beard scratched her lightly, but she was so blindsided by the unexpected embrace that she held on for dear life, her fingers pressing into his bare shoulder blades, her internal temperature skyrocketing as Brody's tongue parted her lips and sought out hers.

Stop this, her brain said.

Just one more minute, her very happy libido argued, getting a sudden charge from the kiss, as if she'd been hit by a lightning bolt.

She couldn't help but smile into his kiss. This was Brody. He was never what she expected, but whatever happened around him, it was always good. At least, it had been.

Hope flooded her. He was glad to see her. Very glad.

"*Excuse* me," an annoyed voice hissed somewhere behind them.

As Brody released her, breaking the kiss, Hannah found the source glaring daggers at her over his shoulder.

Tall, busty blonde, dead ahead.

Brody kept one arm around her, which was a good thing, because Hannah's knees were definitely suffering from a slight wobble.

"I'm so glad you're here, honey," Brody said to Hannah, dripping with his own special brand of charm. But something about his tone hit her as fake; it was the tone he often used around groupies. "Jackie was just leaving."

Hannah saw the other woman's fingers clench. Angry, icy gray eyes and thinned lips emphasized her displeasure as Jackie looked Hannah up and down.

"Who is this?" Jackie asked Brody as if not hearing the dismissal.

"This is the reason you need to go," Brody said simply, delivering a kiss to the top of Hannah's head.

Hannah tried to step away—clearly she had walked into the middle of something awkward—but Brody's muscular arm held her fast against him.

The tension thickened as Brody and the blonde stared each other down for a few seconds.

Brody won.

The woman grabbed her bag from the table and came to the door, standing only inches from Hannah.

"Jerk," she spat back at Brody before she stalked out, marching to a white Mercedes that Hannah had parked beside.

The door closed, and Brody let out a breath.

"Good timing, sweetheart. Maybe that will finally get her off my back for good," Brody said, dropping his arm from her shoulders and retreating through the foyer.

Hannah was immobile, still warm from his kiss as she watched through the window as the blonde kicked up a cloud of dust on the road that led away from the ranch.

"Wait. What the...?" Hannah sputtered.

She was pretty sure that the heat rebuilding in her system wasn't from the kiss, but from anger.

"Did you just use me to get rid of a woman who'd spent the night?"

He looked at her from across the hall, leaning laconically on the door frame.

"She didn't spend the night—not last night anyway. Come on in and have a muffin. There's coffee."

He headed into the recesses of the house. Hannah followed him. She was starving after her overnight drive, and lured by the aroma of coffee. She stopped in the kitchen and watched him pour two cups.

She also noted the half-empty beer bottle on the counter near the sink. Several empties, in fact. While the outside of the farmhouse was pristine, the inside was a wreck, as if no one had cleaned in several weeks. There was also some funky odor coming from the trash basket near where she was standing, so she moved. It was like the house of an eternal frat party. Brody was far from a neat freak, she knew, but he wasn't a total slob, either.

He grabbed several muffins and took the food and his coffee into the adjoining dining room. Hannah's stomach growled. She needed to eat something more substantial than muffins, but a fistful of carbs would tide her over. She grabbed the other mug and a blueberry muffin with coffee-cake crumbles on top.

In the dining room, she took a seat across from Brody at the long harvest table. She had to clear a spot to do so, moving old newspapers and takeout boxes that were stacked everywhere. When she was done eating, she seriously contemplated getting another muffin, but sipped her coffee instead.

"Are you even going to ask why I'm here?"

He looked at her over the top of his coffee cup. "I know why you're here. You obviously needed some more top o' the line Brody lovin', right?"

Hannah coughed, her coffee going down the wrong way. When she caught her breath and started to protest, Brody chuckled.

"Calm down, Hannah. I'm teasing. So, why are you here?" he asked dutifully.

Hannah shifted in her chair, frowning. In spite of the kiss at the door—which had obviously just been for effect—he seemed distant. The connection she'd always had with him wasn't there.

Something was off, and suddenly she didn't feel comfortable asking him for his help. Not until she knew what was going on.

"I was in Atlanta, and I thought I'd come down and see how you were doing. Just a lark," she said. It was mostly true. "How's retirement?"

"You had business in Atlanta?" he asked, ignoring her question.

"Sort of," she hedged.

"'Fess up, Hannah." He sounded irritated. "Did Reece send you here to check on me?"

She sat back. "No, why would he?"

"He seems to think I'm not dealing with my retirement or my accident well."

Another surprise. "What accident?"

He cursed as he leaned forward and shook his head. The gesture made him look even more tired.

"I forgot how to handle a horse. Got thrown, hurt my shoulder and lower back. It's not the end of the world. I'll be fine. Really. I'm just sore and stiff, but mostly better now."

"Oh, I didn't know."

"You expect me to believe that?" he said, pinning her with a look. She could see faint circles around his eyes, a tightness around his lips.

"Are you saying I'm lying?" she challenged him, but now she was worried. She'd never seen Brody like this, and maybe Reece had been concerned for a reason.

He looked away. And then he began to tap his fingertips on the table as if he was holding something back.

"I never knew you had horses," she said, changing the subject.

"There's a lot you never knew about me, sugar," he drawled as he roughly pushed his chair back and returned to the kitchen, apparently done with the conversation.

This wasn't the Brody she'd known. Not by a long

shot. Brody had always been a wild man, a partier and to a certain degree, a player—which was how she'd met him in the first place. But he wasn't ever a jerk about it.

His eyes were bleary, and she noticed now that his gait was off, his walk more hesitant than usual. He held himself stiffly, his legs moving only with concentrated effort, as if each step was painful.

She followed him.

"If you're fine, why is this place such a mess? Are you too hurt to pick up things? Maybe you need a cleaning service to give you a hand?"

He turned on her, eyes narrow, as if his patience was worn out.

"Listen, I don't need help. Just because you and I had some fun together doesn't mean I'm going to spill my guts to you or anyone else. So if that was the plan, forget it."

Hannah took a steadying breath. "Something is wrong. Tell me."

"You don't know me as well as you think you do."

Ouch. Hannah straightened, held her chin high.

"Maybe not. But I'm telling the truth, Brody. No one sent me. But since I'm here, I'm not going away until you tell me what's going on."

Her blog problems fell by the wayside. Hannah knew firsthand that people didn't care as much about their health or their surroundings, or even people they loved when they were depressed. Brody was no dummy; he had to know that she could see this.

Her mother had reacted similarly after Hannah's dad had died, until her mom had gotten some help. Hannah, though only ten, had been the one to take care of the house, the food and her mom in the meanwhile. Brody didn't have anyone, from what she could tell.

She stepped forward, putting a hand on his arm. He flinched, and she pulled back.

"Oh, I'm so sorry, Brody, I didn't mean to—"

His eyes were fierce as they looked down into hers. They were so close, the heat of him burned right through her. She stared at his mouth, her mind drifting back to the kiss at the front door. Hannah had always loved his mouth. She'd enjoyed his smile, his kisses, and many other wonderful things he did with those lips.

"You think you know me, Hannah? You want to help?"

She was unsure, not knowing what to do with Brody in this mood.

His gaze was intoxicating, his body hard and solid. Brody could always turn her inside out with merely a look. Even now, even when he was acting so strangely, that still held true.

"Then help," he said, intention clear in his eyes.

She started to speak, but he stopped her with another kiss. All Hannah could do was hold on.

BRODY'S BODY WAS going to suffer for this later, but he didn't care. Hannah was here.

She was possibly the last person he'd expected to see at the door. When he looked into her sweet face and had her back in his arms, at least one thing about the world seemed right.

He hadn't meant to kiss her again. He was going to send her on her way, but now here they were, and she was making those soft sounds she tended to make when she was turned on.

Even as he deepened the kiss, he tried to tell himself to back off. Hannah didn't deserve this. She didn't deserve his lies or to be the answer for his frustration and restlessness. She didn't need to be part of this sham he was involved in.

Any minute now, he would cut her loose and show her the door.

Or to his bed.

There'd never been anyone like Hannah, and all he wanted was to have her again. To lose himself in her body and forget about everything for a while. Being with her was the last time he could remember anything really good, and he wanted that back more than he could say.

He bunched his fingers in her thick, dark hair— shorter now, and curlier. Angling her mouth so he could go deeper, he walked her back toward the wood island that dominated the center of the kitchen. It was lower than the counters and would work for what he had in mind.

He kept kissing her—Hannah loved lots of kissing—as he covered one full breast with his palm, feeling the nipple bud against his palm.

"Damn, I missed this," he muttered against her lips, tweaking the hard bud between his fingers and catching her gasp with another deep kiss.

She was wearing jeans, and he slid his hand down, working the snap with one hand. Slipping his hand inside, his fingertips brushed her soft curls. He laid his palm flat against her lower belly.

She murmured something against his mouth, but

he continued the kiss, tasting more. He was hard, getting harder. He hadn't felt this alive in some time.

This was what it had been like between them since the first time they'd met: spontaneous combustion.

He slipped his hand between her legs and swallowed her responding sigh. She tried to move against his hand.

"Not yet," he whispered against her ear.

He used his other hand to push her shirt up, moving the lace of her bra out of the way at the same time.

Hannah had the prettiest breasts he'd ever seen. Full and perfectly shaped, the pert, peachy nipples were like dessert to him, and he savored each one in turn.

She cried out, and he saw her grip the edge of the island tight. His back was starting to ache, so he removed his hand and got onto his knees, working her jeans down her legs as he went.

Then he spotted it—the small racing flag tattoo that he'd talked her into, right beneath her belly button. He leaned in, kissed it and looked up to find her watching him.

"You kept it."

"Of course I kept it."

He smiled, remembering the day when she'd gotten the tat, and how they'd celebrated after, made him even hotter.

He nearly lost control then, as he kept looking into her eyes. Hannah, who was so cool, collected and composed most of the time. His responsible, serious Hannah, who wore boring suits and talked about accounting, now looked back at him with wild hair, flushed cheeks and eyes glittering with desire.

But there was more than desire there. There was warmth, need and…affection? Expectation? Concern?

He'd seen that soft look before, and wondered if they had more between them. That was a problem—then and now—because they couldn't have more than sex. Sex was all he wanted. All he needed.

That was an even better reason for her to go.

He couldn't do this, use her to entertain himself, to take his mind off his life for a little while. Brody backed off, his breathing heavy, shaking his head.

"I'm sorry, Hannah. This shouldn't have happened," he said stiffly, closing his jeans as he walked to the sink, washed his hands, his face. Washed the past few minutes away.

"Brody?"

"Just leave, Hannah. Please."

Hannah fixed her clothes, straightened her hair. She still looked amazing and turned on. Brody peered out the window, fighting for control.

"I'm not going anywhere until you tell me what's happening."

"There's nothing to talk about, can't you get that? I'm fine. I don't need you here. Despite what you might think, you mean nothing to me."

He heard her sharp intake of breath. It was low for him to speak to her like that, but he needed her to go. If he had to insult her to get her to do it, fine. It was better than insulting her even more by letting her stay under false pretenses. By taking her here in his kitchen, with no plans for anything more than that.

He didn't warrant her concern, and he certainly didn't want her pity.

"Listen, whether you like it or not, I'm your friend. I want to help, whatever the problem is."

He watched incredulously as she stormed over to the small dinette, sat down and looked at him. He'd never seen such a stubborn, determined woman.

There was only one thing to do.

"Fine, *I'll* go, then," he muttered, grabbing his hat and keys. He walked out the back door, letting it slam, hating himself in about a dozen ways.

He felt like dirt. He wanted to apologize, to beg her forgiveness or to go back and finish what they started.

But he couldn't do any of those things.

Climbing up in his Charger, he wasn't even sure where he was going. All he could think about was Hannah and all the memories of their time together.

As for why she was here—it didn't really matter. He'd still have had to turn her away rather than lie to her. Brody wondered how long it would take before she'd give up on him and take off. He hoped it was sooner rather than later, because he wasn't sure how well he could hold up if he saw her again.

3

HANNAH WOKE UP on a strange sofa, not knowing where she was for a moment, but the faint irritation left by Brody's stubble on her skin brought back the events of the morning, quickly reminding her of her surroundings.

It was midafternoon the same day, Friday. The house was quiet, and she stood, stretching and then looking out the window. Hers was still the only vehicle in the driveway.

Brody was no doubt waiting her out, but in truth, she was waiting him out, too. She had her own stubborn streak, and... Well, she was worried. She didn't want to be, but she was.

Her stomach growled again, and she caught sight of her hair in a mirror on the opposite side of the room. She looked as though she'd crawled out from under the couch, and she seriously needed a shower. Heading out to her car, she grabbed her bag, and then went in search of the main bathroom.

As she undressed and stepped under the hot water, she firmed up her resolve. Hopefully, she'd have a chance to talk to Brody again, but if he wasn't home by breakfast the next morning, she'd go. She could leave him a note with her phone number and an invitation to call her if he needed her—in a purely platonic way, of course—which would put the ball in his court.

It took practice, walking away, making boundaries, but she was getting better at it.

Abby always said she was overly responsible. Hannah never really understood that before; a person was either responsible or not. You either did the things you were expected to and made sure you kept your promises and were there for the people who needed you, or you weren't. How could someone be overly responsible? It was like saying rain could be too wet. Impossible.

But Hannah knew when she'd returned from her month with Brody that Abby was right.

Her employer treated her like crap because Hannah was so dependable. So responsible. When her father died, Hannah had tried to take his place from a very early age. She worked as soon as she could, helped her mother in any way possible. She never wanted to disappoint.

Content to let her hair air dry in the Florida heat, she hung her towel neatly, then threw on a sundress and sandals. She packed up her supplies and went downstairs in time to hear the doorbell ring.

That couldn't possibly be Brody—why would he ring his own bell? Struggling with whether she should answer the door, she did, and found a very pretty young woman in a very scanty cotton summer dress on the other side, holding a pie.

Her pretty smile collapsed when she saw Hannah.

She pushed up on her tiptoes, looking over Hannah's shoulder.

"Is Brody here?"

"No, I'm sorry, he's not."

The woman narrowed her eyes for a second, as if trying to assess whether Hannah was being honest.

"I brought him a pie."

"That's nice. I can put it on the counter and let him know, if you'd like me to."

"Oh, I'd rather do that myself," the woman replied, taking a step forward, but Hannah gently blocked her path.

"I'll be happy to take it for you, or I'm sure Brody will be back later if you want to return."

"Well, I suppose I could leave it. Tell him it's from Jenna, *J-e-n-n-a*. And I'll be sure to make sure he got it," she warned Hannah in an overly cute Southern accent.

As if what? Did she think Hannah was going to eat the pie herself? Or pretend that she'd made the pie instead?

Hannah met Jenna's fake smile with a super sweet one of her own as she closed the door, inhaling the scent of the buttery crust and…cherries. Oh, yum.

Maybe she *would* eat it.

Though after muffins for breakfast, she needed some real food, and pie didn't quite fit the bill. Hannah doubted Brody had anything edible in his kitchen, given all of the takeout bags. Surprisingly, she found the refrigerator fairly well stocked and the cupboards, as well. Someone had gone grocery shopping. One of his many female admirers?

The bigger problem was the kitchen itself, she

thought as she took note of the mess. She couldn't cook in this chaos; she could barely find a clear spot where she could put the pie down.

She tried to resist it, but as she started straightening up, her compulsive side took over. It was part of her nature. She cleared clutter and bounced back and forth between that and putting a pot of meat sauce on the stove to go with some pasta she found in a cupboard.

As she worked, the phone rang twice—two women left syrupy messages for Brody, then a third female caller left one that was rather X-rated.

Hannah huffed a laugh. She wasn't completely surprised. Brody's reputation as a ladies' man—and that was the polite term for it—was quite well established when she met him. It was part of what attracted her to him, actually. He was wild, different and very, *very* experienced.

She'd wanted to be with someone like that to create a few memories she could carry into old age once she settled down. She hadn't been disappointed. When they'd been together, she and Brody were exclusive, even though he'd had offers rolling in steadily, and Hannah had been the recipient of many bitter female glares. Not unlike the one she'd received from *J-e-n-n-a*.

After a while, the place was looking better, homier, and the sauce smelled amazing. Hannah felt much calmer. She was looking forward to her dinner in the now-tidy kitchen when someone walked in the back door.

It definitely wasn't Brody. Instead, a slim, petite honey-blonde stood gaping at Hannah.

Wow, this one had nerve, waltzing right in.

"Can I help you?" Hannah said, offering a cool glance that she hoped cautioned the woman about entering any farther.

"Yeah, is my brother here? I need to talk to him."

"Brody... Um, no, he isn't here. He left this morning, hasn't been back. I don't know where he went."

The woman regarded Hannah with open suspicion.

"Who are you, then, and what are you doing cooking dinner if he's not here or coming home soon?"

"We had an argument, and he took off. I'm waiting him out," Hannah answered matter-of-factly. "But I needed to eat in the meanwhile. And the place was a mess, so I cleaned up a bit."

"Okay. That's either really admirable or really scary."

Hannah realized that she sounded like a stalker.

"I'm sorry," she said, rushing to explain. "I'm a friend. Brody and I know each other through Reece Winston and his wife, Abby? I'm Abby's best friend. I don't know if you know—"

"I do. I know Reece pretty well, though I only met Abby once."

"Brody and I spent some time together last year, at the track, and I was in the area, so—"

The other woman's eyes suddenly widened. "Oh, wait, you're Hannah? *The* Hannah?"

"I guess. Is there more than one?"

"Could be. Anyway, I'm Brandi."

"Nice to meet you. So...Brody mentioned me?"

Hannah felt silly asking, but the words slipped out before she could stop them.

Brandi's lips twitched as she looped her thumbs in her jeans. "Oh, you could say that. When he was under the influence of the drugs they gave him at the hospital when he fell off the horse, you were a very frequent topic. But I won't share details since he wouldn't have, either, except that he was pretty out of it."

Hannah's jaw dropped, her face heating as she tried not to imagine what Brody might have said about her. After a few seconds, she saw the humor in it and started to laugh. Brandi joined in.

Soon, a more serious thought occurred to her. "Can I ask, is everything okay with Brody? He didn't seem like himself."

"I agree. He hasn't wanted to talk about much since he retired from the circuit. He just sort of sticks around here and works on the ranch, but doesn't say anything about what he's doing next. Believe me, we've tried, but it's like poking a bear most of the time. Our parents think he just needs time and space to adjust, but I'm not sure."

Hannah nodded. "I was surprised to hear about his accident, though he seems to be recovering. Still, he does seem…off."

"He is. Anyway, I'm sorry I thought you were another, well, you know…"

"Oh, I know. Believe me. There was someone here this morning, then that pie was dropped off by another young woman, and a few phone messages since… I thought you were, um, a female friend, as well."

Brandi rolled her eyes. "It's as though they come out of the walls. You'd think they would lose interest since he retired, but it's been even worse. I guess they all want to be the one who finally snags him. The one who brings Wild Brody Palmer to heel. It didn't help that one of the reporters let leak something about him wanting to settle down."

"Oh, I didn't know that."

Brandi grinned. "Believe me, if there's anyone less likely to settle down on this earth, it's Brody. I don't even know why he retired. At first we were glad. It was getting hard on my parents, watching him take his life in his hands every day. Whenever there's a crash, we all hold our breath, you know?"

Hannah did know. Being at the track was exciting, but it had also been frightening, watching what he did for a living.

"But he's not happy, especially since his accident," Brandi added with a sigh. "Maybe you'll have better luck at getting him to say what's been bothering him."

"It is hard to imagine him no longer racing. Didn't he and Reece talk about owning their own car, having their own driver?"

Brandi shrugged. "Maybe, but Reece has settled into the winery, and Brody's never been one to sit back and watch."

That sounded exactly like Brody, and it made Hannah wonder, too: Why had he retired? He'd never talked about it when they were together, except to say "in the future" or "in time." Retirement had been forced on Reece because of a horrific accident on the track. That hadn't been the case for Brody.

Unless there was something none of them knew. Was he keeping a secret? Was he sick? Worse?

Hannah's mind reeled with new, awful possibilities. Something so serious that he wouldn't want to tell his family or friends? And that was why he was so surly?

"Anyway, whatever you have on the stove there smells great."

"Thanks. Just some sauce and pasta," Hannah responded, still distracted—and even more worried—by her dire thoughts. "Would you like some?"

"It's nice of you to offer—Brody said you were nice—but I have to get home to my son. I'll catch up with Brody tomorrow. Good to have met you, Hannah."

"Same here."

Brandi left through the back door and Hannah had her dinner alone. She distracted herself by working on her writing and enjoying a bottle of wine. By the end of the evening, she was deflated by the fact that no one was responding to the blog. She hadn't taken any pictures that day, and Brody was nowhere to be found. For the first time since being in New York, she didn't have anything new to post.

Brody said you were nice.

Nice. Bland. Boring.

Like her photos.

Maybe she should call her blog *Hannah's Lack of Adventure.*

As she stood and paced, she noticed a display case on the far side of the room. There were trophies and awards, of course, from his racing, and pictures of Brody with various celebrities, friends, and even one with a US president. A scale model of almost every car he'd raced sat on a shelf.

There was a section of the wall devoted to these shelves. Mostly family pictures and personal items. Brody, she assumed, as a boy with his father, holding up a huge fish. His enormous, toothy grin made her chuckle. He must have been around seven, she guessed.

Hannah had been ten when her father died, and she still felt a slight, dull pain when she thought about it. He'd been a good man and the moon and the stars to her. Her dad had been the kind of solid, dependable man she'd hoped to find for herself. He'd farmed his land, provided for them and worked part-time at the local feed store in summer to earn extra income.

She remembered him as always being happy and laughing, telling her to work hard and do what was right. Those words had stood by her when he'd had a fatal heart attack, and there was no way she and her mother could keep the farm. So Hannah had done the right thing and worked diligently to support herself and her mother as soon as she was able.

She reached out, touching the picture of Brody with his dad. He'd never said anything about his family, which made sense. Theirs was a particular kind of relationship.

Not a relationship at all, really.

There were also some scouting badges—another surprise—and several sports awards, including high school baseball and college swimming trophies. On a table near that display were pictures of Brody in mountain-climbing gear with a group of people all clearly celebrating some sort of victory, and one of him…surfing?

And there were pictures of a very young Brody by a race car—his first one? He had to be only twenty or so.

She'd only known him as a champion driver, but clearly there was a lot more to the man. He'd done and accomplished a lot. She looked at some of the framed news articles and magazine covers. Words that came up often were things like *brash*, *risky*, and *pushing the edge*.

Brody said you were nice.

What did Hannah have to put on her walls? Her diplomas, certainly, and she was proud of those, along with her certified public accountant recognition. She had some pictures from school—mainly her and Abby and a few other friends having fun in Ithaca and at the senior dance. A few 4-H awards from the local fair. Not that she was ashamed of any of those moments— she held them dear, in fact—but in her thirty years, what else had she managed to accomplish?

Her work had been her focus. Creating the stable, perfect future that she had always planned on. She'd be thirty-one in a few months, and she had no job, husband, kids or house.

And here she was, cleaning Brody's place and making him dinner and wondering why everyone, even the strangers on her blog, only thought of her as nice.

Maybe it was time to do something that wasn't so nice? Something daring and un-Hannah-like.

The question was…what?

BRODY'S HEAD FELL back against the headrest of the seat when he saw Hannah's car still in his driveway. Man, she was stubborn. And caring, warm, generous, gorgeous, sexy, funny… Brody bit off a curse, making himself stop there.

He didn't want to lie to her. If he'd been a bad bet before, he wasn't anyone Hannah would be interested in now. She needed security, stability. He'd never been a poster child for either quality, but that was especially true at the moment.

He could only think of one way to convince her to go. It was dangerous, but it was his only play, really. Entering the house through the back door, he stopped short for a second, taking in the gleaming counters and lack of clutter. Something smelled mouthwatering, and his gaze traveled to the pot still on the stove. There was a pie on the counter and he walked over to read a note next to it—"Jenna dropped this off."

Brody shook his head, and then he checked the messages blinking on the phone in the kitchen. He kept the landline precisely so he could screen calls like this; only friends and family used his cell number. He winced, thinking about Hannah overhearing the messages, especially the last one.

Since the nightclub story, he'd gotten several offers like that. Weekly.

Speaking of Hannah, where was she?

"Hannah?"

He walked farther into the house and discovered her sitting on his sofa, quiet, staring at her laptop. There was a bottle of wine—half-finished—and an empty glass on the table next to her. When he came in, she just looked up at him.

"Oh, hi," she said, her brow furrowed as she turned her attention back to the computer screen.

That was all.

"Are you okay?" he asked.

"No. I'm boring."

Brody didn't know what he expected, but it wasn't that. He assumed she'd be ticked off or concerned or whatever, but this threw him. So he went over and sat next to her, and saw on the screen, a page about…

"Why are you reading about alligator wrestling?"

"Because it's exciting and crazy, and risky. Meaning, all of the things I'm not. A decent photojournalist needs to take risks. So I found this place that teaches people to alligator wrestle, and it's not far from here. Do you know about it?"

"Hold on a second. You mean you're actually considering learning how to wrestle an alligator?" Brody's tone was incredulous, but he couldn't help it.

Wait. *Photojournalist?* Hannah was an accountant. Wasn't she?

"How much wine did you have, Hannah?"

"Only a few glasses. See, on the website, they take you through it step-by-step. Here's a picture of a woman doing it, so it's not just for men," Hannah said, pointing.

Brody looked at the screen. "She's twice your size—and a game warden, according to the caption, Hannah. Have you ever seen a real alligator?"

"No, but I have to do something, and soon. You can't help me, and people aren't going to look at my blog for pretty pictures of ocean waves or… Hey, wait. Do people surf down here? There are sharks, right?"

Brody put up a hand, interrupting her. "Let's back up a few steps. One, why do you think you're boring? Two, why are you trying to commit suicide by wildlife? And three, what's this about being a photojournalist?"

She took a deep breath and poured some more wine. Brody suspected she'd had enough, but she was a big girl.

"I quit my job," she said after a swallow, and then told him the whole story, showing him her blog and some pictures of oyster farmers and kids in a decrepit playground in Atlanta. She was pretty good, and he was about to compliment the pictures, but she slammed the laptop shut.

Brody was stunned at her ferocity. He was also somewhat ashamed of himself for having had no clue that Hannah was going through all of this. He was so busy focusing on his own issues that he'd assumed everything with her was status quo—which was how she always liked it.

But apparently there had been some big changes. That had to be why she had come here. Out on the road, on her own, she'd been looking for a friend, and instead he had… Brody rubbed his temples with his fingers, completely disgusted with his previous actions and how he'd spoken to her.

She was worried that he wasn't okay, even though she was having her own professional crisis.

"I don't know what else to do," she said in frustration, standing, albeit unsteadily, as she walked over to his display case.

His grandparents had started the case, keeping everything he acquired since the time he was a kid, and Brody had added to it after he'd bought the house. Some of the things he'd thought about donating to Jackie's auction, but he found most of the items were too difficult to part with. They represented the life he loved. The one he hoped he hadn't left behind him.

"You see? All of this? All the things you've done? *You* know how to live adventurously. *I* do not," she said, sounding totally disgusted with herself.

Brody ran a hand through his hair, unsure what to say. He'd had a plan, but with Hannah three sheets to the wind and obviously in the middle of a personal crisis, all bets were off.

"Hannah, take it from me, you are *not* boring," he said, trying to find some foothold in this weird situation. "You're...exciting in your own way."

As he heard the words come out, he regretted them instantly.

"No," she argued. "I'm not. The only time I've ever done anything exciting was with you."

She walked back over, standing a few feet in front of him, her eyes taking on a softer quality. "Do you remember how exciting some of it was, Brody? Like that time at the track, with all of those people around—"

Brody swallowed hard, remembering all too well. Vividly, in fact. How he'd kept the pretty sounds she made quiet with his mouth as his nimble fingers had made her come behind the bleachers. It had been after a great qualifying race, and when he'd gotten out of the car, all he could think about was making his way to her and celebrating. They'd done that a lot, and it had been one of his best seasons.

"Why did you retire?" she asked bluntly.

"Um—"

"I knew it. You're sick, aren't you? How bad is it?"

Her eyes welled and her lip quivered and Brody stood, pulling her in close and wrapping his arms around her.

"No, honey, I'm not sick. I promise."

"Really?"

"Yes. Except for my back, which is getting better every day, I'm healthy as can be."

She pushed back, looking up into his face.

"Then why? And why are you here, so unhappy and not cleaning up?"

Brody shook his head, fighting a small smile at her focus on the mess. His cleaning lady had moved, and he wasn't motivated to find another one. But that was unimportant.

"It's complicated. Let's focus on you right now."

She made a noncommittal noise, her eyes dropping to his mouth. She licked her lips, and Brody had to hold back a groan.

He and Hannah had had some pretty good times now and then after they'd both finished a bottle of champagne or the like, but this was entirely different. He wasn't about to take advantage, though it was really tough to keep his head straight as her hand slipped down over the front of his pants, squeezing.

"Hannah, oh, um, hon. Let's get you to bed."

"Be adventurous with me again, Brody," she said, pushing up on her toes to drag her tongue along his lower lip as she touched him in a way that made his head spin.

"Hannah, this isn't a good, um, idea," he managed, closing his eyes as she touched and kissed him as he walked her to the stairs.

"I'll show you how good an idea it is," she responded in a purr.

Brody helped her up the stairs, his body liking what she was up to way too much for his own good. She was testing his control.

He deftly steered her into his room and set her down on the bed.

"Aren't you going to take my dress off?" she asked prettily.

Brody looked down at her, his entire body hard, wanting. Her hair was mussed, her lips parted in the most delicious way. The dress she mentioned was pushed up on her thighs, and Brody knew how soft she was underneath.

He walked over to the other side of the bed, lowering himself down, fully clothed.

"Come here, Hannah. We have time. There's no rush," he said.

He gathered her up next to him, torturous as the contact was, since he had no intention of giving her what she thought she wanted.

"You feel so good. I missed you," she murmured against his chest, and Brody closed his eyes.

He didn't say another word, but kissed her hair and stroked her shoulder until her breathing evened and eventually, something he'd forgotten, she offered a soft Hannah snore.

Extracting himself quite gently, he pulled the sheet up over her and left, closing the door. He'd sleep downstairs—after a very cold shower—and hopefully by morning he could figure out what the heck he was going to do.

4

HANNAH WAS MORTIFIED as she glanced out the window at her car, sorely tempted to make a run for it before she bumped into Brody. She couldn't believe she'd practically begged him to have sex with her the night before. He must think she had really come to him desperate for more of…that.

She'd awakened in his bed—still dressed and alone—but she hadn't drunk nearly enough to have forgotten what a fool she'd made out of herself, or what a gentleman Brody had been about it.

Of course, it had to be less than attractive to have a drunk, depressed chick groping you and talking about the good ole days, she thought as she softly banged her head against the window frame. And it sounded as if he had enough of that in his life, from what his sister had told her.

What had she been thinking? *Good going, Hannah.*

Still, there was no way she could up and leave. She at least owed him a thanks and an apology. So she took a deep breath and went outside. He had to be around here somewhere, since his car was still parked in the drive.

On her way across the driveway, she rehearsed what she'd say. She'd thank him, tell him that if he did want to talk, she'd leave her number. That would be that. As she approached the path that led down to the barns, she had to stop and admire the sleek muscle car he drove. It defined power, she thought. It was made for speed and taking charge.

Hannah had never really cared about cars one way or the other until she'd hung around Brody and the track for a month. She still didn't understand all of the intricacies, history, and all the models and so forth. She did understand, though, how people could connect with a vehicle on a very visceral level.

She and Brody had connected on the hood of his stock car once, and the memory made her feel warmer than the early-morning heat could be blamed for.

Hannah turned her attention to the beautiful grounds as she walked along the path. Quiet and peaceful, the only sounds came from birds and the whinny of a horse down in the barn. The rolling fields were a mixture of mowed lawn closer to the house, wildflowers, then longer grass and bushes beyond, all surrounded by mature trees, many of them draped in the Spanish moss she'd always thought was so pretty. It provided a nice mixture of sun and shade over the area.

She stopped and smiled with delight as she saw a small deer about fifty feet away, nibbling at some moss. It didn't seem to notice her, content as it ate its breakfast.

She wished she had her camera; it wasn't an exciting picture, but it sure was cute.

Figuring Brody was down in the barn, she continued in that direction. Indeed, she did find him inside, tending to several horses.

She paused for a moment in the entrance, loving the cool air that was thick with the smell of hay, wood, horses and hot summer. It reminded her of her childhood. She swallowed the hard lump in her throat as she watched him secure a lead rope around the neck of a beautiful red roan.

The interplay of muscles in his arms didn't escape her attention, either, nor how his obvious strength contrasted with the gentleness he exhibited with the animal. He conversed with it in low tones, smiling as the roan seemed to answer his comments with snorts and nods.

As the horse fully emerged from the stall, Hannah saw it was a mare, and a beauty at that. She loved horses, and she'd had one of her own when she was very young, but they'd sold it with the farm, which had been one of the most heartbreaking parts of her youth. There was no room for a horse at their apartment in the city, of course, and renting stable space had been financially impossible then. The new owners had let her come back to ride the horse now and then, but it wasn't really hers anymore.

Abby and Reece also had horses, and Hannah loved taking them for a ride or even helping out in the stables. Still, she never expected to find Brody with equine. She supposed in some ways it wasn't such a surprise; Brody was drawn to powerful things.

Fast, potentially dangerous things, she thought with a smile.

"She's gorgeous," Hannah said, making her presence known.

Brody turned, greeting her with a smile.

Well, that was a good sign. Hannah relaxed, stepping farther into the barn. Having the horses as a buffer helped somewhat, since she still wasn't sure what she wanted to say to him.

"This is Sally," Brody said, petting the horse's nose.

"Hi Sally. You are such a sweetheart," Hannah crooned, putting her hand out to the horse, who promptly stuffed her nose into her palm, snuffling for goodies.

"And who is this?" she asked, walking farther down the aisle and lifting a hand to another horse's nose.

"Zip, meet Hannah. Hannah, meet Zip," Brody said with a sidelong look at the horse.

"Nice to meet you, Zip."

The horse nodded his head in greeting, snorting.

"Of course. They told me he was a ladies' man," Brody said as Zip nuzzled Hannah's fingers.

"He's absolutely beautiful. They all are," she said, looking at the curious heads poking out over their stall doors. "But he's...special, isn't he?"

"That's one word for him," Brody teased, chucking the horse gently on the chin and receiving a tolerant huff in response.

"Were you taking them out to the pastures?"

"Yeah, they all go out for most of the day, then I clean up the stalls."

"You don't have people to do that for you?"

"I don't mind the work. What else do I have to do?"

Hannah bit her lip, unwilling to pry at the moment, though his tone gave her another hint at his frustration.

"I'll take him for you, if you want to go with Sally. I could help with the stalls, too."

"That's not a good idea. I know you're around Abby's horses a lot, but Zip is… Well, as you said, special."

Hannah understood immediately from Brody's tone. "He's the one who threw you?"

"Yeah, and he enjoyed it, I'm pretty sure."

"He does have a sparkle in his eye," she said, grinning. "But I can handle him. He'll be fine, walking out."

Brody hesitated, but finally nodded.

"You take Sally—I'll get him and we'll take them out together. We'll be fine, Brody."

He relented, handing her the tack while he returned to Sally, who waited patiently. Hannah forgot the awkward encounter she'd been expecting and enjoyed the distraction.

She kept a firm hold on Zip, Sally on the other side with Brody. As she walked the thoroughbred, she let her shoulder gently bump up against his, like buddies walking along together. He seemed to like it.

She liked him, too, but she also couldn't help but be aware of the power of the horse. He walked as though he was barely holding back from bolting. It was much the same feeling she got from Brody a lot of the time, especially now. Strung tight, needing to be let loose.

"Where did you get him? I can feel the energy

practically coming off him in waves," she commented as they walked out into the sunlight.

"Thoroughbred rescue. He has a very impressive racing pedigree, but he was too unmanageable, so they surrendered him to the rescue when they couldn't sell him. I know the owner of the rescue, and she knew I had open stable space. They wanted me to keep a few of their horses for a while, but they weren't being adopted, so I took them on permanently."

Hannah smiled. "That was a very kind thing to do, Brody."

And more like the man she'd known, too, she thought to herself.

"He's a bit...touchy. I was working with him, but he might need a better hand than mine, clearly. Jed will probably do better with him."

"Jed?"

"He helps with the farm, has ever since my grandparents lived here. He's excellent with horses, and he's been working with Zip a bit each day since I hurt my back."

Hannah nodded as Brody opened the gate to the pasture. He led Sally in, but told Hannah to wait.

"Zip goes over in a separate section—he has to until he's gelded anyway."

"Ouch. Poor Zip," she said with a comforting pat.

"We're hoping it will calm him down some."

"You don't sound entirely convinced," she commented as they walked to the next corral.

"Well, you know...I sort of like him as he is, but I also don't want him hurting himself or anyone else. I'm waiting to see how he responds to more training, but if we're going to geld him, I want to do it before he gets much older."

Hannah nodded, led Zip into the smaller pasture next door to Sally's and then walked back out with Brody, leaving the horses, her buffer, behind.

"Um, listen," she began, taking a breath as they walked back to the barn. "I have to apologize for last night. I was…in a weird mood, and I guess the wine really lowered my inhibitions," she said with an embarrassed laugh. "But thank you for, well, being so considerate."

"I owe you an apology, not the other way around. I wish you'd told me about your situation."

She smiled at him. "Talk about pot and kettle."

He laughed. "Well, we'll call it even. As long as you promise not to go wrestling alligators or sharks."

She laughed ruefully. "That's an easy promise to make."

"You feel like a ride? The other two horses in the stable need some exercise. Zip and Sally had a ride yesterday, but Salty and Pepper—my parents' horses—need some exercise. I'll put Snow, the other rescue, out with Sally. She's older and just likes wandering around the pasture. Then we could go out on the trails for a bit."

Hannah knew she should say no. She should say goodbye while things were settled and agreeable.

Instead, she looked up into Brody's face, admiring the laugh lines around his green eyes and the way the sun played off reddish highlights in his brown hair. She liked the angle of his chin and his nose, and she especially liked his mouth. She liked his hair longer, and less severely cut. It suited him.

He looked better today. More rested. Had she been imagining how bad off he'd seemed to her the day before? Maybe she'd made too much of it?

"I was planning to leave after we talked," she finally said halfheartedly.

"You can still go, later." His eyes dropped to her mouth as he said the words, making her shiver.

"That's true," she agreed, knowing she was rationalizing, but so what? It wasn't as though she had to answer to anyone about how she spent her time. No schedule to keep. New Orleans would still be there.

Brody turned back toward the barn, motioning for her to join him. Hannah paused before she did so, enjoying studying his other assets as he walked ahead of her, a smile twitching at her lips.

She met his parents' horses, who were older and so impossibly sweet that Hannah fell in love with them immediately. Salty was a female white draft horse, and Pepper a mostly black quarter horse.

Salty was immense, and gave Hannah pause for a second, but the mare was a gentle girl and didn't mind at all being saddled. In fact, she seemed eager to go.

"We can head down through the trails on the back of the property—it's a nice, easy ride, and cooler under the trees," Brody said as he pulled himself up on Pepper.

"You're okay to ride?" Hannah asked, thinking about his back.

"I'm fine, particularly on these two. When it comes to Zip, I probably can't ride him for a while. I can't risk screwing up—uh—you know, making my back worse than it is."

He sounded disappointed, and Hannah didn't find

that surprising. Of course Brody would want to get back on the horse that put him in the hospital. Riding Zip was probably akin to riding in one of his race cars—and potentially as dangerous. But he also sounded as though he had been about to say something else and then changed his mind.

What was Brody afraid of messing up? Did he have some kind of new venture in the works?

They headed toward the tree line at the edge of the corrals where a path opened into woods that were almost like a fairy-tale setting. Moss draped from trees, and tall pines weaved in between those, all blocking the heat and layering the dirt with a soft path of detritus where the needles lay. Hannah felt as if they had been transported back in time to some ancient forest.

Sun danced through the trees, illuminating a thatch of wild orchids, purple thistle, pine lilies and other plant species that she didn't recognize, but they were beautiful all the same. A few insects buzzed by, but there were far fewer mosquitoes than she would have expected, and she mentioned that to Brody.

"We sprayed last fall, which cuts them down in spring, but also, it's better during the day. At night, especially midsummer, it can be rough."

The horses seemed to know their way without direction as she and Brody rode side by side without saying too much except for noticing things along the path here and there. Brody shared a few family memories with her, a tree where he used to hide so he could jump down to scare Brandi, or a secret hollow where he'd hid boyhood treasures. He seemed more relaxed, and she was, too.

Time melted away, and eventually they reached a

point where the path widened out around a pond that was deep green and covered in water lilies. Frogs were singing all around, their baritone croaks making her laugh.

"Mating call," Brody said with a grin and a wiggle of his eyebrows, making her laugh.

A small stone bench sat at one end of the pond, and they dismounted and let the horses rest while taking a seat.

"I can't believe this is all yours. It's like living in a national park," Hannah said. "How did you ever manage to leave?"

"I spent a lot of time here as a kid. My parents lived on the property next door. They moved to a condo ten years ago, but this was a great place to be a kid, for sure. But once I made my first drive around a track, all I wanted to do was drive every second I could."

Hannah nodded, pondering. Turning to face him, she tried to ignore the romantic setting, the moist heat that suffused the air. Brody looked incredible, as though he had walked out of a fairy tale himself. He was strong, virile and so very sexy. In spite of his back injury, he was clearly in fine shape. Very, very fine.

What she was feeling must have shown in her face, because his eyes darkened, his hand reaching out to slide over her shoulder, pulling her closer. The next thing she knew they were kissing, his fingers diving into her hair, her mouth meeting his hungrily as her hands slid over his chest.

"We should stop," she managed to gasp as he buried his face in her neck, leaving a trail of hot little nips and kisses there. She let her head drop back, wanting more. Stopping was the furthest thing from her mind.

"I know. I can't seem to get near you without wanting to touch, and taste," he murmured against her skin. "You don't know what it took to walk away from that bed last night."

One hand drifted down to her chest, palming her breast before circling her peaked nipple with his fingers, and she groaned, pressing into him.

Her heart was slamming in her chest as she realized that right now she wanting nothing more than Brody as deep inside as she could get him. Right here, right now.

"Are you going to walk away from me this time?" Hannah challenged, pulling back slightly to look at him.

Brody's gaze bored into hers, his chest rising and falling faster, his jaw tense as he shook his head.

"I don't want to, but you might, after you know the truth."

BRODY KNEW HE was about to send Hannah packing. It was for the best, he tried to convince himself. He wanted her, and he couldn't be around her for five minutes without acting on that desire.

It wasn't good for either of them. He should have let her say her goodbyes at the barn. That would have been the easy thing to do, but easy never was his preference.

And...the truth was that he hadn't wanted her to leave. The whole time they'd been riding along, making small talk, he'd been trying to find some sane way to have his cake and eat it, too—to maintain his secret and have Hannah in his bed—but that wasn't possible.

He either slept with her while lying to her about

his situation, or told her the truth and watched her leave. Again.

Both options sucked, but at least if he told her the truth, he wouldn't hate himself as much later.

"What do you mean? The truth about what?" she prompted. Her eyes widened and she looked worried. "Are you really sick? Brandi said she didn't know why you would have retired, that you refused to talk about it with her or Reese," she said hurriedly, putting all the wrong pieces together, so Brody shook his head, stopping her.

"No, I promise, I'm *not* sick, but…there is a special situation. What I tell you, Hannah, it has to stay between us. You can't tell anyone, not even Reece or Abby. No one."

Her pretty brow crunched, perplexed. "Okay, but why? If you aren't sick, then what—"

"I didn't retire. Not really," he responded quickly. "It's a…it's a publicity stunt, basically. To rebuild my image, make me more appealing to the fans. The sponsor was going to drop me if I didn't straighten up after the sex-club scandal. I sit out this season, lie low, live a quiet life and then they'll stage a comeback for the new and improved Brody Palmer."

Hannah was quiet, settling back on the bench, and Brody wasn't sure what she was thinking. It was a relief, he had to admit, to tell someone the truth. Keeping it to himself had been difficult, but what would she say? Brody had always made a point of being a straight shooter, and now he was lying to everyone he knew.

After a long pause, she said, "How could they force you to do that?"

Brody took a breath. "They're my biggest sponsor, and without them, the other sponsors would probably drop out, as well. I could try to finance the team myself, but not indefinitely. So I went along with it. It's not as though they were wrong—my image was a little rough."

He braced himself for Hannah's no-doubt scathing response, but it didn't come.

"So they basically blackmailed you into this?" she asked, the sides of her pretty lips turning downward.

"No, not like that. Well, I suppose it sounds that way, but it's been done before. It's actually more of a second chance, I guess. It was my choice, ultimately. I could have said no, but…I want back into racing. I'm not ready to quit yet."

"But the only option would have been to lose all of your sponsorship or to quit? That's not fair," she responded, looking angry on his behalf. Brody stared at her in amazement, not having expected that response.

He didn't know if he would ever be ready to quit racing. Was there anyone, anything, he wouldn't sacrifice to get back in a car? Certainly, it had been easy enough to let go of his integrity.

"Well, I appreciate that, but I still had a choice. I made this one."

"So you have to hang out here and not get into trouble?"

"More or less," he responded with a nod. "Though I wasn't doing a very good job. Being home has been…tough. I spent some time getting the farm renovated, getting the horses, but I was bored out of my skull. I ended up going back out, drinking a little too much. Then there was the accident. I thought I'd lose my mind in the hospital. Then somehow it got out that I was retiring and looking to build a life, wanting to settle down. It caused a whole bunch of other problems."

"That's absurd, them trying to control your life like that! And your family—they don't even know?"

"They can't know. I shouldn't even have told you, but…with how things are with us, I couldn't let *us* go any further without your knowing the truth. I also didn't know if you might have thought, since I was retired, you know…that things could have changed," he said with some degree of embarrassment. "I couldn't sleep with you and let you think that, well—"

Realization dawned. "That marriage was a possibility. You couldn't have me thinking *that*."

"Yeah, but I realize that's not why you came here now. I'm sorry about that. I completely understand if you're upset," he said, waiting for the moment when she would get up, walk out and tell him to go eat dirt. "But I don't care about the others, or what they think. I do care about you, Hannah."

"Thank you, but I wish you had told someone. Reece would have understood, surely."

"Maybe. But it's not only about me, Hannah. A lot of people's livelihoods all depend on this. My team, the people who make what I do possible. I owe it to them to keep my mouth shut. If even one word of this leaked, it could leave a lot of people hanging out to dry."

"Wow. You really are in a tough spot."

Brody blinked, wondering why she still wasn't

marching off, telling him off or giving him the cold shoulder.

"So you see, we can't be together, because… Well, things are complicated right now."

"I guess the sex-club story was the one that broke the camel's back with your sponsor?" she asked, her voice lower. The sidelong glance she sent him was hot with curiosity, as if she wanted to know what he was doing at a club like that.

"Yeah, they knew the truth, but it didn't matter."

"The truth?"

"Someone I know, a married friend, was there, and he got in a bind. I went to help out and the press showed up, so I covered for him and took the flack instead. I thought it would roll off, given my history, but not this time. That club has a reputation for being particularly kinky, and it was too much for the sponsor to swallow."

"So…you weren't there because you're into anything, um, different?"

"Disappointed?" he asked, lobbing a challenge back in her direction, watching her blush slightly, which intrigued him.

"When I saw the news report, I couldn't help but wonder if there was something about you I didn't know. Maybe things you liked that you thought I hadn't been adventurous enough to try."

He shook his head resolutely. "Nothing like that. I never held back with you when we were together. Believe me."

She smiled slightly at that, and the kick of desire it delivered made his heart stutter. Was there something Hannah was thinking about that she'd like to try? Some secrets she was keeping?

Brody trained his mind away from the thought.

"So I'm the only one who knows?"

He nodded.

"I would never tell a soul, Brody," she said, reaching over to put her hand over his. "But…"

Here it comes.

"Maybe I could help. Maybe we could help each other. I have an idea."

That wasn't what he expected at all, and he stared at her blankly.

"Help each other? How?"

"I can see now why you've been acting like you have. You need to clean up your public image, right? And you've been fielding all of these…pies," she added with a mischievous grin. "So what if I stayed a while? What if you said we were back together? That would make your sponsor happy and stop other women from coming around, right?"

Brody was completely confused now.

"Why would you do that?"

"Well, because…I want you," she said, the admission warming her cheeks as she slid him another cock-hardening look. "I know that you're absolutely not interested in commitment, and I'm not looking for it, either," she said resolutely.

"Hannah—"

"No, really. That was the reason I came here. I needed *your* help. I was focused for so long on settling down and living this perfectly structured life, and where did it get me? Quitting my job was only the first step. I look at my blog, and I see that nothing I'm doing there is exciting because *I'm* not doing anything exciting. It's time I did. I thought if I could blog about your retirement—"

"Hannah, you can't write about this on your blog, I—"

"I know that. I promise, I won't tell anyone. But maybe you could show me how to live a more adventurous life? Teach me how to take more risks. I could blog about that instead."

"Hannah, sweetheart, believe me, you are plenty exciting, and I'm probably not the best—"

He didn't get further than that, since Hannah levered herself up and over him faster than he could get the words out, planting a hand on either side of his face and lowering her mouth to his.

Her kiss was different—she took control, coaxing him, pressing into him and showing him that she meant what she said. The effects sizzled in his every nerve ending. Her tongue stroked his, muddling his thoughts as he splayed his hands on her hips, letting her have her way. He couldn't remember what he was saying before.

When she pulled away, she nipped his bottom lip, looking down into his eyes, her hair falling in her face, her eyes sparkling.

"Believe me, you *are* the best," she said with a chuckle, drawing one from him, too.

"That's not what I meant."

"I know, but what do you say, Brody? I can be your stabilizing influence," she said with a naughty smile. "And you can help me learn how to live more dangerously. I don't want to be the same old Hannah.

All bets are off. I want to be more daring, take more chances—starting with you."

He wanted to say yes more than he wanted to breathe.

But...

"I don't want to hurt you, Hannah. I don't want to take advantage of the fact that you're in a vulnerable spot right now. Maybe you think you know what you want, but—"

She pressed in closer. "If you touched me right now, you'd find me ready for you, Brody. I know what I want, and I want it right now."

"Hannah—"

"I get it. You don't want to hurt me. But I don't need you to protect me. I don't *want* that. I've protected myself from everything for way too long. I thought I could build the perfect life around myself, but I couldn't. I wasted so much time, Brody."

"That's why—"

She didn't let him finish, interrupting with an impatient shake of her head.

"When Reece was racing, he almost died, but he fought his way back. Abby's family home burned to the ground, but then she found Reece and started a new business. She goes to her house in France now, for goodness' sake. You had to put your life on the line every day to race, and then you hurt yourself riding a horse, but you want to get back on the track. Everyone around me takes risks. Sometimes they get hurt. But look at what wonderful things happen, too. I sit and watch from the sidelines. No more."

"There's nothing wrong with that."

"Really? Do you remember when I asked you if

you worry about dying when you get in the car before
a race?" she asked.

Brody did remember. He thought about the safety
of others on the track, and he knew the risks. They
all did.

He also knew that even if he did everything perfectly, something could still go wrong, something out
of his control, but he couldn't get in a car thinking
that way. He had to be all in.

When he got in the car, all he thought about was
winning. Facing the unknown was part of the excitement. That was what he'd told her.

And right now, all he wanted to think about was
Hannah.

He understood what she was saying, and so he did
what she asked. Pushing all of his reservations, worries and what-ifs to the background, he tugged her
closer. He'd walked away from her twice now, and
he wasn't going to do it again.

Brody snugged the V of her thighs against his erec-
tion and pressed upward, grinding into her. The sound
she made in response, the way her lips parted, her
eyes getting soft as her cheeks warmed, sealed the
deal for him.

Leaning forward, he found the hard nub of a nipple,
bare under the soft cotton of the T-shirt she wore, and
closed his lips around it, drawing through the fabric,
making her moan as she pressed back against him,
her fingertips biting into his shoulders.

He wanted her naked, now.

But this was Hannah's moment, and as much as he
wanted to take her, he pulled away, reclining against

the hard back of the stone bench. He pinned her with a look, loving how undone she was already.

He raised an eyebrow and smiled a challenge.

"Okay. I'm all yours, Hannah. In public, you can be my very well-behaved girlfriend, but in private… whatever you want, however you want it. If you dare…"

5

FOR A MOMENT, Hannah's thoughts blanked. It was so easy to hand over control, to get Brody to agree and then let it happen, but clearly he wasn't playing that particular game.

No. If she wanted this—really wanted it—she was going to have to take it.

He was calling her bluff—not that it was a bluff, really, but it had been words. Now he was telling her to make good on them.

You can't think about failing—you think about winning, Brody had once told her. At least in his world, the results of failing could be fatal. They'd all seen crashes, seen friends and competitors hurt, and worse. He'd said that the pressure was so intense that if he thought about it too much, he'd never go out on the track in the first place.

Her second thoughts lasted less than a second. Her smile met the challenge in his eyes.

Hannah *wanted* to win. Big-time.

"Oh, I dare."

Pushing everything else out of her mind and focusing only on the rise and fall of his chest, the way his hardness fit perfectly against her sex and the hunger that fed the challenge in his gaze, she leaned in and kissed him again.

It was a small kiss, almost chaste. Light, teasing and slightly naughty when she flicked her tongue out to taste him before standing up from the bench and stepping back.

Brody sat up, looking pensive. Wondering if she was changing her mind?

No way.

She grabbed the bottom of her T-shirt and peeled it over her head, throwing it at him as she let the sun filtering down into the glade play over her bare skin.

Hannah had never been completely naked outside before, in a place where someone could see her. Granted, there wasn't anyone here except for the horses, but who knew? Maybe someone would come looking for Brody or appear on the path, out for a walk.

Even if the risks were imagined, they still sent a thrill through her as she unbuttoned her jeans, shimmying them down her legs while watching Brody's expression grow taut with desire.

His eyes took her in as if he'd never seen a naked woman before, and that egged her on. She turned around, facing the pond, slipping her panties down as she bent slowly to take them off, one foot then the other and then threw those back at him, too.

Primal female joy rose inside of her as the slight breeze teased her exposed skin. She lifted her face to the sky, imagining herself as some magical wood nymph. Brody cursed under his breath.

"You're so beautiful," he said.

Turning to face him, she smiled.

He didn't make a move except to watch, his eyes devouring her. He was letting her call the shots.

So she did.

Crooking her finger, she beckoned him in a manner as old as the ages. He stood, walked to her, and she took the edge of his shirt, pulling it up and over his head, throwing it onto the bench with her clothes.

Then his jeans, boxer briefs, boots...until he was naked there with her. Gorgeous and male, every strong muscle and angle exposed to her touch. She took advantage of that, exploring him thoroughly in the dappled light, lips chasing fingers until he was hard, jutting against her, trembling.

She was, too.

But a bite of sharp reality cut through the diaphanous haze of her desire when she remembered they were away from the house, away from—

"Wait," Brody said roughly, reading her thoughts.

He turned to the bench, fishing something out of his jeans, cursing a few times as his fingers, clumsy with need, fumbled and his wallet fell to the ground. Then he turned back to her with what she'd thought they were missing.

"Oh, yes," she said with heartfelt gratitude.

She took the packet from him, covered him. He was familiar in her hands, and yet this all seemed new. Unknown.

That was the end of sanity for them both.

Hannah turned to face the pond, and Brody's arms came around her from behind. His hands covered her breasts as he buried his face in her shoulder at the same time he planted his cock deep in her sex, making her gasp, her body reacting around his.

Brody moved in long, slow strokes, pushing her higher as she bent back to press her lips to his for a deep kiss.

Hannah could feel the pleasure coiling, ready to strike, and murmured to him to stop. He did, and she motioned him to the bench, to where he'd been sitting.

Hannah grabbed her jeans and his to cushion her knees from the stone surface of the bench, crawled up over him, planting her hands on the back of the sturdy seat and then took him, deep and sure.

This was *her* win. The first of many, she hoped, setting a pace and losing track of everything.

As he thrust up into her, their cries and moans merged with the breeze and quieted the songs of the birds and frogs for several long seconds until the only sound was their breathing, filling the glade with sweet gasps.

Hannah collapsed over him, spent and slick with sweat, muscles almost too lax to think of ever standing up again.

It had been too long. Far too long without this. Without Brody. Even though it wasn't their first time together—far from it—it was different.

Because she'd gone for what she wanted. Accepted the dare and hadn't looked back.

She was giddy, and she immediately wanted more.

"I should have dared you more often," Brody said, finally finding his voice as he hugged her closer.

"I wish you had," she said, linking her arms around his shoulders. "I hope you will."

Their skin cooled and Hannah unlinked her arms,

putting space between them as she sat back on his thighs, reluctant to get dressed. This was like a dream that she didn't want to let go of. Already, she was having a difficult time believing she'd been this bold.

"I guess we should get going," she said, her fingers meshed with his.

"Let's maybe swim first?"

"Oh, that would be lovely," she said with a smile, letting him lead her to the clear green pond. Pretty white lilies floated on the surface, and Brody stood at the edge, holding her hand and gazing down into the water.

"Worried it's cold?" she teased.

"No, double-checking for gators," he responded seriously. "But we're good to go."

Hannah blinked in surprise, but let him pull her into the cool, clear water, gasping as they surfaced after submerging.

"This is wonderful," she exclaimed, looking up at the sky through all the trees that surrounded them, cupping a lily pad in her hand and smiling at Brody. "It's as though we're lost in some tropical world."

"It does have that feeling," he agreed as he dived underneath again, his hands sliding up her legs and making her laugh as he pulled her back down under for a kiss. They relaxed and swam in the cool waters for a while, before it really was time to head back.

Emerging from the pond, the warm air dried their skin almost before they put their clothes on. When Hannah pulled herself up into Salty's saddle, she bit her lip, loving the way her oversensitized body felt every bit of pressure from the saddle, the movement of the ride reminding her what had happened only a few minutes ago.

It had not been a dream.

But as they rode down the path, single file as the greenery closed in, her thoughts started to churn again.

Maybe her deal with Brody was as crazy as it sounded, but Hannah needed to do something crazy. Playing house while he faked his retirement was completely the opposite of anything she'd ever do. Which was what made it absolutely perfect.

She wasn't in denial. Hannah knew she'd probably get hurt—at least a little. Being with Brody was addictive; it had been before, as well.

Or maybe she wouldn't get hurt. She wanted to become adventurous, not tied down. She had to be sure to keep that in mind.

Finally, they emerged into the light of an open meadow and pulled up side by side again. The barns were in the distance, and Hannah looked at Brody, her serious thoughts receding.

"Race back?"

He looked pensive, but then nodded. Before she could say another word, he nudged Pepper from a walk into a run, and shot ahead of her before she could shout, "No fair!"

Laughing, she held on tight as Salty took off as well, but they weren't able to catch Brody. He stood in the shade of the barn by a trough, letting Pepper drink while she and Salty caught up.

Hannah shook her head as she slid down from Salty, leading the horse over to the water.

"You play dirty, Palmer," she accused playfully.

He grinned. "You snooze, you lose," he teased.

They led the horses to the stable, where they washed and brushed them down before taking them to a shady part of the pasture. Hannah was surprised to see several large birds moving among the horses, pecking at the ground.

"What are those?"

Brody secured the gate behind the horses.

"Guinea fowl. My granddad brought a pair decades ago for pest control—they will eat every tick and mosquito around, and even clear out snakes. They kept multiplying and have been here ever since. Every now and then, when they overpopulate, we'd take one for Sunday dinner, but otherwise they just roam and keep the pastures and fields pretty free of pests."

"Wow…I didn't know birds could do that."

"Yeah, chickens are good for mosquitoes, too, I guess, but we never really planned on farming birds. The Guineas seem to be more or less self-sustaining."

"They *are* pretty fierce looking," she commented as one ventured closer.

"You should see them face off over a snake. They probably scare the things to death."

"You get a lot of snakes?"

"Mostly rat snakes, but some copperheads. The rat snakes are actually good to have around, too, but the birds don't think so."

Hannah shuddered as they walked back to the house. "I can't imagine any snake being good to have around."

"Afraid of snakes?" he asked.

"I was bitten when I was small. By a copperhead, in the Adirondacks. My father took us out camping to

this island in the middle of a lake. You could only get
to it by canoe. I was bitten, and we had to paddle back
to the car to get to the hospital. I was in such pain. I
was only seven, but I can still remember how bad it
was. So, yeah, no snakes for me, thanks."

"Aw, babe, that's awful."

His arm slid around her as naturally as if they'd
been together for years, and her heart fluttered in
her chest. Maybe more than it should as they walked
back to the house.

"So how does this all work, do you think?" she
asked.

"What do you mean?"

"Our pretending to be a couple? For how long do
you think? A few weeks? A month?"

"Are you sure about this, Hannah? I thought you
were traveling around, seeing the country. Why do
you want to be stuck here? It might take a while to
convince someone we're in anything permanent."

"I need your help, Brody, and so it makes sense
for us to help each other. I know the score. You help
me with my lack of adventurousness, and I make you
look like an upstanding example of the male gender.
Clearly, I have my work cut out for me."

Her tone was light, but there was a sinking feeling in her chest that it might not be that easy. Second
thoughts and worries started to crowd her thoughts,
but she pushed them away.

That was old Hannah. She'd made her decision—
no backing down.

"Okay, well, we could talk more about it, and play
it by ear on how long we'd have to keep it up. I suppose we should make some public appearances, let

people see us together, and I should probably tell Jud I've met someone so they can stop pestering me about it in the news," he said, still sounding hesitant. "It will mean media appearances, Hannah. You know that, right?"

Hannah the introvert cringed inwardly, but Hannah the adventurer nodded confidently.

"It will be good exposure for me. And maybe fun... and good exposure for the blog. I've never been interviewed before."

"Okay, as long as you're sure. It is the perfect solution for me, and if I can help you, I will. But if you want to go, you should, anytime you want. And you get to be the one who dumps me, even," he said with a grin.

"I figured as much," she answered cheekily.

As they approached the house, the sound of tires grinding on the loose rock of the drive drew their attention, and they turned in unison to see a van approaching, parking a few yards away. A slim blonde with her long hair tied back in a high ponytail slid out, a guy with a camera exiting the other door.

"Damn," Brody muttered under his breath. "Well, we're about to jump into the deep end. If you want out of this, say so now."

"What?" Hannah asked, watching Brody's expression tighten at the same time his arm around her shoulders did. "Who is that?"

"Marsha Zimmer. We call her Marsha Stalker as a joke, but the woman is not funny. She's the one who broke the story on the sex club, and she's been on me ever since. I can't seem to turn around without her being there."

"Who does she work for?"

"Tampa news. She's a junior reporter, but she's got sharp instincts. She's been smelling blood in the water about this retirement thing, and it's been a job trying to keep her out of my face. She wants to move up the ladder, and she's not shy about stepping on whoever she has to."

"Sounds like a sweetheart."

Brody grunted in response as Marsha approached them.

"Brody, nice to see you looking well," she said, her eyes traveling over him in a predatory way that made Hannah's jaw clench.

"I don't think we had an interview today, did we, Marsha?"

"No, but I was in the area, and I hoped to confirm a few rumors before I went with my latest story—"

"That would be a first," Brody said.

"Now, now. Play nice," Marsha said, clearly not fazed at all, from what Hannah could see.

Then the reporter's gaze homed in on her. Yikes.

"You look familiar," she said, narrowing her eyes, but clearly not able to remember.

Hannah had never been interviewed when she was with Brody before, but there had been some published pictures of them together. Hopefully that could work for them now. Hannah hoped her smile looked natural as she stepped forward with her hand out.

"Hannah Morgan, nice to meet you."

Marsha shook her hand, focusing on Hannah so hard Hannah thought the woman might stare a hole between her eyes, and then Marsha's eyes widened. Hannah could almost hear the click.

"Daytona. You were…hanging out with Brody then. I remember seeing a few pictures of you with the team."

"That's right," Hannah agreed, not saying anything more.

"Well, then, that dispels one of the rumors right off the bat."

"And that would be?" Brody asked.

"That you and Jackie Nelson were pairing up for the charity auction, but Jackie suggested that you were also pairing up for a lot more than that. Considering that you've been out with several women in the past few months, of course, I had my doubts that you would settle down with just one," Marsha said. "But I also heard that you were having trouble with your sponsor and trying to make nice after what happened at that club. In fact, someone even thought that maybe you were fired, instead of retiring?"

Hannah expected that Brody might lose his temper at the woman's goading, but he only sighed heavily before answering, as if tired or bored by the question.

"Jackie and I are friends, Marsha. I'm donating some items to the auction, and we went out a few times in the past, but that's all. You must have misunderstood her."

"Apparently. And as for the sponsor?"

"I don't have a sponsor. I'm not racing. Retired, remember?" he said, as if she were daft.

"Hmm… Well, I figured you'd never take yourself off the market. Wild Brody Palmer, settling down with just one woman? Puh-leese," Marsha said with a not-so-friendly chuckle.

Hannah linked her arm through his, keeping her voice steady. "Well, that's where you're wrong again, actually. Brody is off the market. He's with me."

"You mean, for this week? This is an on-again, off-again thing, or friends with benefits?"

Hannah bristled at the woman's tone.

"We've both been getting our careers figured out. I needed some time, but when I came back down to see him I knew this time I wouldn't be going back north. I'm here to stay."

Cynical doubt practically spilled out of the woman's eyes as they met Brody's. "Jeez, Brody, all the women I talk to seem to think you belong to them."

Brody tucked Hannah in closer. "But in this case, you won't hear me denying it. Hannah and I had a great time back in Daytona, and when we got together again, the feelings were still there and very mutual."

Hannah could tell by Marsha's face that she wasn't buying it. Not one bit.

"You expect me to believe you were in love with her the whole time you were visiting sex clubs and dating other women? Sorry, Brody, try again. The only way I'd buy this is if I see a ring on her finger or a date set for the wedding," she scoffed.

"Well, we haven't had time to talk about a ring yet, but we were talking about possible wedding dates on our ride today," Hannah said. "Before you showed up unannounced."

That stopped the reporter in her tracks, and she felt Brody stiffen beside her, as well.

"You're engaged? And when did this happen?" the reporter asked sharply, her whiplike gaze snapping to Brody.

"Um, well…it's still unofficial," he stuttered, trying to catch up. "It's brand-new."

Hannah held her breath. He obviously hadn't expected her to go that far, but there was no going back now.

"How romantic! So you only just proposed! I guess that's why you look so…flustered."

Hannah smiled. "It was a spontaneous kind of thing. We're still getting used to the idea ourselves."

"Well, this is my lucky day, then," Marsha said, as though she was licking the cream from the bowl. "I get the scoop."

Brody took a deep breath, swallowing hard as his eyes met Hannah's.

"I guess you do."

"WHAT WERE YOU THINKING?" Brody said, shoving his hand through his hair as he paced the kitchen.

After talking to them for a while longer, forgetting her other stories and getting the scoop on the wedding—they wanted something small, simple and as soon as possible, it turned out—Marsha left, only agreeing to hold the story for one day. Why not share his good news? she argued. He'd begged off, saying he needed time to tell his family and friends first. Amazingly, Marsha, so happy with the story, had agreed to give them until the end of the weekend.

Brody was not as happy.

How was he going to explain this to his parents? They'd been hoping, secretly, that he'd find someone and settle down. But this was only more lies.

"I'm sorry, I couldn't stand how she kept twisting everything and being so snotty. It made me mad,"

Hannah explained. "When she asked, I thought... It seemed like the best way to discourage her, I guess."

"Well, we certainly made her day, but what are we going to do now?"

"Well, this works, right? Your sponsors wanted you to appear like you were putting down some roots, and now women will stop bothering you. It's not real, Brody. I know that. There's no need to look so panicked."

"It was fine to say we were together, Hannah, but now we're supposed to be getting married, and as soon as possible? When we don't go through with that, Hannah, I'll be a liar, or they'll say I dumped you, cheated on you or never meant it in the first place—and I'd like to know where she heard that bit about the sponsor. No one should know about that."

Hannah's smile faded. "She might have been guessing. Seeing if she could hit a nerve. But we can stall. Weddings take time."

"Not small, simple ones."

Hannah put a hand to her brow. "True. I don't know where that came from. She brought out the worst in me. It seemed as though the more details we had, the more believable it would be, and that one slipped out."

"Well, she sure believed it. Now we're stuck."

"We're not, not really. People change wedding plans all the time. We can say we wanted to do it in fall instead, and then—"

"And then I'm back at square one. You don't have anything on the line here, Hannah, but it's my whole freakin' life." He regretted the words as he said them, but still, they were also true.

Hannah sat at the kitchen table, her head dropped into her hands.

"You're right. I'm so sorry. I really backed us into a corner. But we did tell her it was impulsive. Maybe it's not too late to contact Marsha and tell her we spoke too soon, and that we're not sure what we're doing yet, for a wedding?"

"She'd sense something is off—it would make things worse."

He'd had a glimpse back in the glade of who Hannah wanted to be—the Hannah who existed under the gray suits and dark-rimmed glasses. He'd seen glimpses of her before, but he'd also always liked her exactly for who she was.

Brody walked to the sink, leaning on it as he stared out the window, trying to focus. Panic was what killed you, right? He needed to think.

There had to be a way to make this work. A way to make it...

The truth?

Seriously?

He turned to back to Hannah, who had reached for a tissue to blow her nose—she was crying. He sucked in a breath. He didn't want her crying over anything, especially when it came to him.

"Listen, it's okay. Don't cry, hon. But...what if we did it? For real." The words were surreal, and he didn't think she'd heard him at first.

She sat very still, and then turned slowly, her expression a study in total, complete shock.

"What?"

"It would take a day or two to get the paperwork done, and then there's a three-day waiting period, but that's it. Then we would have to schedule a ceremony and whatever else needs to be done."

Hannah didn't say anything, but her horrified look was a clear response. But the longer the words lingered in the air between them, the more his dread was replaced with new energy.

"Listen, like you said, it's not for real. We can still call it quits down the line, whenever you want. This could work," he continued.

The more Brody talked, the more he convinced himself it was the right thing to do. It made perfect sense.

"Are you *insane*?" she finally said.

Brody walked up to her, grinning. "Yeah, but you knew that already. You said you wanted some adventure, Hannah, and to take risks. So…what do you say? Let's get married!"

He'd rendered her wordless again, so he reminded her, "Hey, it was your idea."

She gaped. "It was *not*. I thought we could have a long, fake engagement, which we could drag out, like a lot of people do. Not a real marriage."

Brody shook his head. "I'm already in a fake retirement, and that's been hard enough. And there's no way out of this that doesn't rain all the hell Marsha Zimmer can muster down on my head."

"So you'd rather have a fake *marriage*?" Her tone was incredulous.

He had to admit, when she put it that way, it did sound pretty wild.

Brody liked wild.

"It wouldn't be fake. It would be very real, in every way," he said, sliding his hand into her hair, cupping the back of her neck and making her look at him. "In *every* way, Hannah. Until we decide to end it. What do you say?"

Brody saw the indecision in her eyes, and maybe a hint of panic. But she was also…considering.

C'mon, Hannah. Go for it.

He moved in, pulling her close, his lips against her ear.

"Think about it…you'd be the one who caught Brody Palmer," he teased with a smile and a kiss on the shell of her ear. "No one would ever think you were unadventurous again. And it *would* be an adventure, Hannah…whatever you want to do, however you want to do it, I'm there," he whispered, echoing what he told her back in the glade.

Her breath caught as he nipped at the soft flesh of her earlobe, and desire quickened again, fed by the excitement, the wild thrill of what he was proposing— literally. He felt her response, too, as she softened against him, her breath hitching slightly.

Married to Hannah. He played the idea over in his mind as he smoothed his hands over her back. He'd never really considered marrying anyone. Maybe when he was a lot older, if then, but for now, his career came first and he was happy playing the field. A very wide, diverse field. He couldn't blame Marsha for thinking about him like she did; she wasn't wrong. Brody enjoyed women, lots of them.

That would change. Even if it wasn't a real, forever marriage, he wouldn't mess around. He never did that, not even with his lovers. And when he was with Hannah, he never thought about anyone else anyway. Not then, not now.

And this wasn't a forever thing. It was a "for now" thing. A mutually beneficial arrangement. They had a built-in escape hatch, anytime either of them wanted out. His name, his connections could open doors for her, maybe help her establish herself somehow. It could work. Like she'd said earlier, they would make it work, for both of them.

In fact, in his mind, it was as good as done.

He started to kiss her again, but Hannah pulled away, turning away from him, wrapping her arms around her middle.

"I don't know, Brody. I hear what you're saying, but for me, it's a much bigger lie."

The words cooled him down quickly.

"How so?"

She shrugged, walking over to the window where he had been standing before.

"It's one thing to stay here for a while, to be lovers…but I always loved looking at my parents' wedding pictures, and I imagined I'd have pictures like them someday. With the dress, the flowers… Happy memories my kids could look back on when they were older, too. Marriage is…a promise. It's not a business arrangement. If you have a way out before you even start, it's not real on anything but paper."

Brody nodded, meeting her eyes. "You're right, I know. My folks have been together almost thirty years. And maybe someday you'll have that kind of marriage, too, right? You can still have all of that. But you said you didn't want it now. That you wanted to change how you've always locked yourself down and that you've been too focused on a particular kind of life. I'm not a forever kind of guy, Hannah, you know that."

"Yes, I know, but—"

"Even though the marriage would only be temporary, it wouldn't be a lie. I do care about you. I want you, and I enjoy being with you. We're good together. It could be the answer for both of us. It would help me with my public image, get Marsha and everyone else off my back. And I could help you break out of your rut, help your career. Give you time to figure out what's next. Isn't this exactly what you were suggesting to me earlier, only with more paperwork?"

She chewed her lip, clearly unsure, but he knew she was listening to him.

"This could be fun, Hannah. A lot of fun," he added, seeing that she was almost with him.

"I must be as crazy as you for even considering it," she said, shaking her head.

Now her eyes lit with that same spark he'd seen earlier. Brody made a silent promise to himself that he'd only encourage that spark, make it shine brighter. If he couldn't give her forever, he could give her that.

He met her at the sink, pressing her against it, not giving her another chance to rethink anything as he took her mouth in a hot, open kiss that promised nothing but more of the same.

When he was done, she was breathing as hard as he was and was as ready for more.

"Will you marry me—for a while—Hannah?" he asked again.

She took a breath, giving him a look that made him feel as if she was handing him the world.

"I must be nuts, but…yes."

6

"You what?" Abby screeched. "Are you kidding me?"

Hannah had to hold the phone from her ear for a second, but her smile was wide as she listened to her best friend's response to her announcement.

After she'd gotten over the initial shock of the entire incident, she realized Brody was right. Her resistance to marrying him for real, sort of, was because of the attitudes she'd held about the institution since she was young. It was the bastion of stability she'd always aimed for, and if there was one way to blow that bastion to bits, it was getting married—temporarily.

It all made her feel reckless and young, but that didn't mean that she wasn't also nervous about telling her friends and family. Brody was taking her out to dinner with his parents in a few hours to break the news to them.

First thing that Monday, they'd gone to get the paperwork settled and scheduled the following Friday afternoon at the local courthouse, which was the earliest date they could get. Brody suggested Vegas, but Hannah nixed that right away. Vegas was too cheesy, and if what he needed was the impression of permanence and commitment, that wouldn't work.

Brody agreed that their wedding needed to look as real as possible to the outside world, but Hannah had quailed at a church wedding with all the fuss—that was too much, especially if they wanted a short engagement—so a small courthouse wedding with family and friends was the compromise. It also kept Hannah's ideas about her real wedding someday intact—she wanted to have the church wedding with all the trimmings when it was for forever.

This would do for now.

She had yet to tell her mother, and that had made her feel somewhat guilty. Still, she had to have her mother at her wedding, no matter what the circumstances.

"Yep," she said to Abby. "Pretty soon, I'll be Mrs. Brody Palmer. Though I think I'll probably keep my own name, actually."

She thought of that at the last minute—she wasn't about to change her name when this wasn't a permanent thing. So many details to consider, even in a fake marriage.

Or rather, a *temporary* one, she corrected herself. A shiver ran down her spine as she remembered Brody's voice when he told her how their marriage, for as long as it lasted, would be very real in *every* way.

"So how did this happen anyway? I need to know everything," Abby said, getting worked up. "And you guys should be married here, and have a party at the winery—if you wait three or four months, which is like *nothing* in wedding time, it will be summer, and it would be lovely. And what about a dress? Does your mom know?"

Hannah waited until her friend ran out of breath and then took the questions all in their turn.

"We can't, or rather, we don't want to wait months, Abby. We want to be together now. Officially. Maybe we can do something this summer, come up there for a visit. Mom's phone went to voice mail this morning when I called, so don't say anything. I still have to tell her, too."

Abby blew out a breath, and Hannah could imagine her shaking her head.

"Hannah, I don't know. I love Brody, but he's… *Brody.* Not exactly Mr. Monogamous, and to say this is fast is an understatement. Do you think that you might be reacting to the loss of your job? And he's been a mess with his retirement… Maybe I shouldn't have sent you down there. Things are so uncertain for you both—marriage is something you should think twice about in any situation, but especially in yours."

"I know it's fast and unexpected, but that doesn't mean it's not right, Abby. Remember, we aren't new to each other. All of those feelings were there before, I guess, but I was too blinded by tunnel vision about what I thought my future should be. I didn't realize I would still feel as much for him—more, really—as I did before."

Hannah's chest tightened as she found her explanation perhaps a tad too convincing, too real for her comfort. But she was plunging forward, a new Hannah Morgan, who didn't stop and rehash every emotion and consequence.

"But—"

"Do you think Reece will get back from France in time? I know this is very short notice, but we'd love you to come."

"Hannah, I don't get it. This isn't like you, not one bit, and it's different from everything you ever said you wanted."

Which was exactly the point.

"I know. But when you find the right guy, the rest is not as important, I guess."

"I suppose…but still. I'll call Reece right away. I know he'll be as upset as I am if we can't make it, but either way, you have to come here as soon as you can so we can all celebrate. Reece and I are throwing a huge party in the summer, it's going to be like racing-world heaven here, so get used to the idea."

Hannah laughed, but for the first time, genuine tears stung her eyes, and she had to wait a second to respond, trying not to be too emotional.

She failed, and both women ended up laughing and crying on the phone, until Hannah hung up, needing to call her mother again and then get ready for dinner out. With her future, temporary in-laws, whom she'd never even met.

Real nerves set in for a moment as she dialed her mom's number and shared the news—rehashing a lot of what she'd gone over with Abby, and then more happy tears. She and Brody would pay for her mom to come down, of course, and she could stay at a bed-and-breakfast by the beach, also at their expense.

"We'll let you know as soon as we have the details set, Mom," she said.

"Are you sure, honey? I could come down earlier on my own, help with any plans and arrangements?"

"We're keeping things very simple and small, so there won't be too much to do. We'll have a ceremony and then take everyone to dinner. We can't expect you all to rush and do everything when we're springing this on you."

Her mom agreed—albeit reluctantly—but when Hannah hung up the phone, she didn't feel very good about it. To distract herself from her uncomfortable thoughts, she picked through her suitcase, getting to the bottom and realizing she had nothing really appropriate to wear to dinner with Brody's parents.

He came in as she was picking up the mess of clothes she'd thrown everywhere.

"How'd it go with Abby? Can they make it?"

"Fine. She's going to try—she has to see if Reece will be back in time. And I have nothing to wear to meet your parents," she said, clearly panicking. "Nothing. We can't meet with them tonight. I need to get to a store to find something appropriate. Maybe tomorrow night would be better—"

Brody placed his hands on her shoulders, stilling her diatribe.

"Anything you wear will be perfect. Don't worry. They're going to think you're amazing, like I do," he said, planting a kiss on her forehead.

"Did they see the news report?"

"Of course. I called them right before they saw it on the lunchtime news, but it was close. They're surprised but happy. I guess there's not much I do anymore that surprises them," he said with a self-effacing chuckle.

Brody loved his parents—she could tell by the look

of warmth in his eyes when he talked about them. That made her feel somewhat better.

"But as it turns out, you have a reprieve," he continued. "I thought you might need some time to get used to the idea, so I rescheduled for tomorrow night."

Hannah took a deep breath of relief. "That's good, thank you. I want to make a positive impression… they're your parents after all. Your sister knew—a lot more than she should, so she told me—about our month together back in Daytona, by the way. You were chatty under anesthesia?"

Brody winced. "Right, the hospital—sorry. But that can work for us. Make it all more believable, which is the point."

"So your parents probably know, too, that I'm *that* Hannah," she said, with the same emphasis Brandi had used. "I don't want them thinking, you know, that I'm some gold digger or not good enough for you."

Brody's expression couldn't have been more shocked. "Are you kidding me?"

"It's what Brandi thought at first. Why wouldn't they think so, too? This *is* somewhat out of the blue, and it's not as if they know me."

"They'll think the obvious. That you're a warm, intelligent, funny, wonderful woman, and how could their recalcitrant, misbehaving, womanizing rake of a son have done so well for himself? If anything, they'll think I'm not good enough for you, and they'd be right."

She reached out, plucking a piece of hay from his shirt. He'd been down with the horses while she was on the phone.

"You keep saying things like that and it's going to be harder to divorce you someday."

Brody chuckled again. "Well, anyway, this means we have the rest of the evening free. I had some ideas about how we might celebrate our engagement," he said, hands settling on her hips as he leered over her shoulder at the bed.

Hannah smiled, her stress dissolving as she linked her arms around his neck.

"You're right. I guess I have to get used to this whole being-spontaneous thing. I keep lapsing back into worrying and wondering if it's the right thing to do," she admitted.

"It's going to be awesome," he said, nuzzling her cheek with his.

"Oh, yeah? Prove it," she challenged, her skin warming wherever he touched her and at all points in between.

"Challenge accepted. But I could use a shower first. Want to join me?"

As if she would even consider saying no.

Hand in hand, they walked to the huge en suite bathroom. It was a new addition, converted from a smaller sitting room, and it was stunning.

En suites weren't typically part of the construction in older homes, but this one had been perfectly designed to complement the style of the house. The white marble tile with gray veining alone had to have cost a fortune. Hannah stared at the soaking tub with bubble jets—*that* definitely had possibilities—as Brody went to the huge walk-in shower. She'd looked at a similar tub in a store once and couldn't imagine ever spending that much money on such a thing, even one as gorgeous as this.

"I can't believe I'm going to live here for a while. With that tub," she said more to herself than anyone, and then caught Brody's lifted eyebrow.

"You don't see anything else in here that you like?" he asked, making her laugh again.

Great sex, laughter and that tub.

Worry was definitely the enemy of adventure, and she had to stop it. She focused instead on the man who clearly should have all of her attention at the moment. It was what *he* thought that mattered.

"Well, I love the shower, too. That tiled bench is awesome," she teased, reaching past him to run her hands appreciatively along the smooth surface.

Brody caught her around the waist and pulled her up close. His mouth on hers quelled their laughter. It only took a few minutes for them to leave their clothes on the floor and make their way under the spray of the hot water, which seemed to rain down from every direction.

Hannah barely noticed, though. All of her attention was firmly focused on Brody now as he took a lovely natural sponge from the shelf—he was saying something about it coming from local waters—and filled it with soap. He handed it to her, grabbed another and did the same.

Oh, so nice. They stood close, washing each other, rubbing the soft sponges over her curves and his angles until they focused on more tender, sensitive topography.

He washed her hair, taking his time, turning her to mush at the lavish attention. Then his sponge moved lower, and Hannah whimpered against his shoulder, losing her grip on her own sponge as she rocked into the rhythm. Seconds later she was sagging against him as easy, rippling pleasure washed over her, much like the water that ran down her skin.

"That's it, babe," he encouraged, holding her up with his other arm, which was curved securely around her lower back.

Brody walked her backward until they reached the bench, where she sat, feeling loose and warm, wet all over. But when he took one of her wrists and held it above her head, she perked up, curious.

"What are you doing?"

He took the satin belt from her robe hanging close by, looped it around her wrist and then the other one.

"Too much?" he asked, pausing.

She considered for a moment, but this *was* what she wanted. Everything new, everything different. And as he had told her earlier, she trusted him. At least with her body.

"No. It's okay," she said.

He proceeded to gently tie one wrist, then the other, to the towel rack over her head. Nerves wrestled with excitement.

He stood back, taking his time looking at her. "Brody—"

"Do you know how beautiful you are?"

The words rendered her mute. She didn't know how to respond. No one had ever said things like that to her.

Had Brody said them to others?

She shook her head, as if physically casting off the thought.

"What? What were you thinking just then?" he asked, coming forward and kneeling down, taking one of her feet in his hands and rubbing.

"Nothing important... Oh, that's good," she sighed, loving how his touch traveled through the happy nerve endings, triggering a chain reaction of sparks all the way up her body.

"Tell me," he insisted.

He lifted her foot, kissing the arch before dragging his tongue along that sensitive skin, making her head spin.

"Tell me, Hannah," he said again, nipping her toe.

"Oh, I was just wondering if you said those kinds of things to all the girls," she said, trying to make it sound like teasing.

But he knew better. He knew her.

He stopped, looking into her eyes, dead serious. "I've never been with anyone I didn't like, and I've liked a lot of women... But you're different, Hannah. You always were. You have to know that," he said, switching to the other foot.

"Different?"

"You aren't someone I met around the track or a fan or someone I worked with. You're...normal. Real."

She huffed out a laugh, mixed with a moan as his fingers moved up her calf.

"Boring, you mean."

"No, that's not what I mean," he added, leaning down to nip the tender flesh behind her knee as a reprimand for her comment, making her jump slightly before he licked the spot. "Not at all."

"Ordinary, then?"

"Only in the sexiest, 'I want to peel that gray suit off you' kind of way."

He continued up her thigh, nipping again, and then licking. Hannah found she liked that subtle sting soothed by the kiss, so she egged him on.

"Exceedingly dull?" she goaded, holding her breath for the next touch of his teeth to her skin. Instead, he raised his head, looking at her with molten, knowing eyes.

"Oh, you're very bad," he said in response, parting her legs and moving up in between. "You play the good girl, but you're not, are you?"

His words pleased her immensely, and she shook her head. She wanted to be bad.

"I think you need to pay for that," he said with mock severity.

"Please," she said encouragingly at the first touch of his tongue to the overly sensitized nub between her thighs.

No more nibbles—he tempted her with his tongue until she writhed on the bench. She wished she could sink her hands into his hair and put him where she needed him, but the inability to do so fed her increasing arousal, sending her to the moon.

Hannah might have screamed his name, she wasn't sure. The release he drew from her was so powerful she couldn't do anything as it took over. Waves of climax thrummed through her entire body, the undertow pulling her for as long as it pleased, carrying her where it wanted and pushing her back up to the surface when it was done with her.

As she caught her breath, her body shaking and

spent, she looked down to see Brody watching her, the raw emotion and desire in his expression stunning her.

He grabbed a shaving mirror from the shelf, held it up to her.

"This is what I see in you, Hannah. When you let go, when you're playful and lose control and you do it with me… It's anything but boring."

She looked at her reflection in the steam-edged glass and hardly recognized the thoroughly satisfied woman in the mirror.

"Oh," she said, unable to say anything else as he stood up and gently untied her hands, kissing each palm in turn as he did so.

Brody cradled her against him for a few minutes under the spray. Locking his lips to hers, he pulled her leg up around his hip, slipping inside her so easily and completely, it was perfect.

Hannah held on again as he started moving, loving the connection and the warmth as the shower rained water down over them. She didn't have another orgasm in her after what he'd just done, but that didn't matter. It gave her more time to notice and experience his body, his pleasure, separate from hers. That was a wondrous thing, too, and she memorized every detail.

She kissed his neck, whispering hot things in his ear until he was tense, every part of him hard and ready before he let go on a long moan, his face buried in her shoulder.

Seconds later, as he lowered her leg back to the floor and his breathing slowed, he stilled.

"Oh, I completely forgot—"

She put a hand on his shoulder. "It's okay. I'm protected. And I haven't been with anyone since you. You know, when we were together, before."

He was clearly surprised at that revelation, and the tenderness in his eyes at her bald admission moved her.

"I'm sorry to say I was, but not since the hospital. I was checked out thoroughly and I'm fine."

"Then I guess we don't have to worry about any... barriers, especially since we'll be married after all," she said.

If she kept saying it, maybe it would start to sound real.

"We should still be cautious. Can't have a new addition, given the circumstances," he said.

The words were a reality check in her fuzzy post-coital moment, but he was right. Their situation was what she had to keep first and foremost in her mind.

They stepped out, drying each other off, and the results of that nearly sent them back into bed for more. But when the phone rang, Brody shook his head.

"That's Brandi's ringtone. I should check it. We've been playing phone tag."

"Go get it. I'll forage in the kitchen. I'm starving, and there are probably leftovers I could heat up for us," she said, pushing him toward the door, appreciating the view from behind as she did so.

Hannah hummed and smiled all the way down to the kitchen, mulling over what had happened in the shower. She'd liked it. A lot. More than she would have thought. She wanted to do it again, and she wanted to do more. It was like getting to know herself for the first time in her life, and she liked what she was discovering. It could only get better from here, right?

She rummaged through the fridge and took out the leftover sauce from the day before just as Brody walked into the room.

"We have enough sauce if you have some more pasta, or—"

"I have to go, I'm sorry," he said, tense and looking worried and irritated all at the same time.

"What's wrong?"

"It's a family thing. Brandi's son has been acting out, and she needs me to go find him."

"You know where he is?"

"I have a good idea. He's been street racing, and he's already been picked up once by the cops. They won't let it go if he's picked up again. I shouldn't be long, but I'm not sure. You go ahead and eat."

"I can go with you."

"No, these street races can be in some rough areas—backstreets and bad neighborhoods. It's better if I go alone."

He turned away, planting a quick kiss on her mouth as he headed for the back door.

Hannah hardly had a chance to say another word, but she knew she wasn't a fan of getting the brush-off, especially like that. Especially after everything that had happened between them.

As if she didn't have any part in his life, except when it came to sex. Obviously, Brody didn't understand that making a marriage real meant more than making it real in bed.

Besides, this sounded like something she wanted to see.

Street racing… It sounded exciting.

She heard him get in the Charger and start the engine. Before Hannah could think twice, she grabbed her keys and headed out the door, waiting until he was down the driveway. When she knew he couldn't see her, she followed him.

BRODY PINCHED THE bridge of his nose, hating the stress that had been in Brandi's voice as her plea rang in his head. *Brody, please, find him before he gets killed. He'll listen to you.*

Aiden was supposed to be in his room—grounded, again—when Brandi noticed he was missing.

Brody headed out onto the highway, hitting the gas until he exited a few miles south.

The roads narrowed and closed in, but he knew the area like the back of his hand, having traveled these roads many times in his youth, much like his nephew, when he should have been home studying.

This one led out to an old airstrip in the Everglades, abandoned, just as it had been when he raced there. Brody knew the races still happened—a few times he'd even gone to watch—but he didn't like Aiden being involved any more than Brandi did. However, he did understand it more than his sister could.

It wasn't long before he could hear the roaring engines in the distance, and that took him back, too.

How many times had he sneaked off to race down here in the very car he was driving now? Way too many. Back then, it was different.

He could see them now from the crest of the hill that led down to the strip, the light from dozens of cars illuminating the pitch-dark. They'd also set up some construction lights to brighten the strip, and parties were in progress.

He parked the Charger in a secluded spot at the side of the road and put a jacket and baseball hat he had in the backseat on, walking out into the clearing. There were hundreds of kids here, the cars more expensive and tricked out than any he and his friends had had back in the day.

The use of nitrous and other dangerous modifications was typical these days, and then there was the fact that a good number of these cars or their parts came out of chop shops, bought on the black market, obtained from stolen vehicles. Illegal betting, bookies and even drug runners came to the races to find new talent.

Still, he had to admit, casting an eye over the lines of a sweet Chevy as he walked by, there were some really, *really* nice rides here. And while they were dangerous in the hands of amateurs, he knew more than one professional driver who had raced on the streets before going pro. Some of these kids really could drive.

The bigger problem was the ones who only thought they could, or who thought they'd be able to walk away after rolling a car at a hundred and fifty, brush off the dust like it happened in the movies.

Aiden should know better—his father had been in the stock-car circuit, too, and had died driving to the grocery store one night. He'd had a heart attack at the wheel and couldn't be revived. But Brody suspected that only egged his nephew on even more. It made sense that Aiden would feel close to the father he'd never known by trying to walk in his footsteps, but even so, this wasn't the way.

Brody scanned the crowd for his nephew. Aiden didn't even have a car yet, but that didn't matter. There was always someone willing to lend a ride for the right price. Aiden was here somewhere, and Brody kept to the edges of the action, walking around, appearing to check out the cars while looking for his sister's son.

He heard his voice before he saw him.

"You need to find that line and follow it through, man, like this…"

Brody listened as his nephew offered another kid some advice, waiting until Aiden's friends moved on.

"You forgot to tell him that the trick is being able to find the apex of the curve," Brody said, walking up behind him. "But you know finding that sweet spot is really more about instinct. If he's messing it up, he could do more than lose. He could get hurt. Or worse. You know that, too."

Aiden spun around, his expression clearly frustrated.

"Yeah man, you're busted. Let's get out of here. Your mom's worried."

"No way. I still have my heat to run."

"Not tonight."

Aiden leaned in, almost as tall as Brody now, at sixteen. Brody lifted an eyebrow at the kid's chutzpah. Just like his old man, all right.

"You're not my dad, Brody. Who are you to say? You used to do this all the time. I heard you talk about it once in an interview."

Brody felt some regret for that. It was true. It was

years before, but he couldn't help but feel responsible for unintentionally encouraging an illegal activity. He'd been called out for days after that interview by parents whose kids were street racing. He'd tried to set it right, but what could he say? He *had* street raced, and he'd been honest about it when he was asked. Those days had been some of the best times of his life.

"You're right, but—"

"Don't tell me, it was different back then," Aiden mocked.

"It was. Listen, Aiden, I know you're only doing this because your mom tells you not to—"

"I'm doing this because I *love to drive*. She doesn't get that. She wouldn't even let me get my license."

"What? You don't have your license?"

"I have a license," Aiden said a bit too deliberately.

A license. Probably a fake or stolen one. Brody realized that he had been far too absent from Aiden's life. How could he not have known this? It wasn't good. He understood his sister's reasoning—she was afraid for her son—but it was going to backfire.

"Whose car are you driving?"

"A friend's. I win, we split the take."

Brody shook his head.

"Listen, you come home with me this time, and I'll talk to your mom. We'll get your license, a legal one, and I'll teach you some things. Maybe you can start working on that piece of junk Mustang down in the old barn with me, and it will be yours when it's done," Brody added.

He'd thought of doing that before with the kid, but he wasn't home long enough, usually. "We can even go to the track, but only if you give up the street racing. Completely. Got it?"

For once, Aiden was speechless. Brody didn't know if that was a good thing or a bad one. There'd be hell to pay with Brandi, who wasn't going to go for this idea at all, but she was going to have some hard choices to make, too. She couldn't wrap her son in wool forever.

"You mean it?" Aiden asked, wary in the way only a teenage boy could be.

"I don't lie, Aiden. You know that."

Not about this anyway.

His nephew was about to say something when they both heard a shout from the starting line and saw the flag go down; the sudden roar of the engines and screeching tires distracted them both from their conversation. Brody was as mesmerized as Aiden, watching the cars speed down the strip.

"I *have* to run this heat, Brody," his nephew said. "The money's already set."

Brody shook his head. "Tell me who and how much. I'll settle it."

Aiden frowned, but after a few seconds, he sullenly pointed to a guy standing off the side of the starting line with two girls who looked too young for him. Hopefully, the money was small-time, and he would be able buy out Aiden's stake with what he had on him.

"Hey," he said, approaching the guy, ignoring the two boys behind him who stepped up.

"What you want, old man?"

"I want to buy out my kid's bet. He's going home."

The man laughed, and shook his head. "No way. Once you're in, you're in. He drives or loses the car."

"How about I double his stake?"

"Unless you can pay more than the car is worth, which I seriously doubt, the answer's the same."

He turned to his two girls, effectively brushing Brody off.

Brody stepped around, facing him again.

"What if I drive for him, then? It doesn't have to be him, right? I could take his place."

All of them laughed then. "What's wrong with you, dude? You got money to throw away?"

Brody shrugged. "It's my money. Here. I'll even double down," he said, reaching into his wallet for some bills.

The guy took them, still laughing. "Whatever you want, old man. Which car?"

Brody pointed to the car that Aiden had indicated, and while it wasn't great, it would do.

"Whatever. You're up next."

Brody nodded, walking back to Aiden. His nephew was suitably mortified, but Brody only patted him on the shoulder.

"Take it easy, Aiden. Now you don't have to think of what you would have done if you'd lost your friend's car."

The boy glowered. "I wouldn't have lost."

Brody grinned in approval. He couldn't help it. "I'll be back in a few."

"We'll both be in deep if someone recognizes you. Professionals aren't allowed. It's like cheating at a casino."

Brody agreed. That hadn't changed.

"Well, no one has so far, and I'll be going too fast for them to see me in a few minutes."

He caught the smirk that was nearly a smile on Aiden's face as he headed for the car, and couldn't deny the thrill that always gripped him before he raced. Granted, this wasn't a high-tech stock car and it wasn't a professional track. It was a lot more dangerous, but Brody was up to the task. Especially if it kept Aiden out of the car and out of street racing.

Brody walked around the car, looking under the hood, checking the tires. It was a decent BMW sedan with a few upgrades, but nothing fancy. Good. That would work better. He could depend on his driving, then, not modifications. And if by some chance he crashed, he stood a much better chance of getting out alive.

He wished he had the Charger, though. He'd blow these idiots off the road with that car, but this would have to do. Climbing in, he adjusted the seat, the mirrors and waited until the starting line cleared.

When he pulled up, he looked at the kid next to him sitting in a respectable Corvair, gunning the engine and glaring as if he had a chance.

Brody shook his head and waited for the flag to drop, his fingers flexing on the wheel, good tension invading his limbs as he braced himself for the go.

Just before it did, he saw someone with a camera pointed at the car and did a double take.

It was Hannah.

Spotting him through the lens, she nearly dropped the camera in surprise. Brody lost a half second and started with a lurch as the flare gun went off, the flag coming down and the Corvair getting the jump on him.

What was she doing here…and taking pictures?

He couldn't think about it now, and reined in his focus to drive, getting a quick feel for the car and the shifting, steadily pulling up on the back end of the Corvair. The other car was fast, but the kid's driving was messy and he was shifting too quickly. Driving for sound and not sense, Brody thought, now at his side before they hit the cones at the end of the runway. They both had to circle before returning.

Easy enough.

Until the brat in the other car bumped him.

"You picked the wrong car to play with," Brody muttered.

Bumping was a regular, if criticized practice in racing, as was rubbing, where cars would brush against each other, side to side. It was always risky, but professional drivers normally knew their limits and used the technique strategically.

This kid was just being a jerk. Brody didn't want him to get hurt, but he could play with him a little, too, and did so.

As the Corvair tried to bump again, Brody quickly swerved to the left, and the other car lurched as it missed him, wobbled and slowed down for half a second before getting its pace back.

Speeding up on him, the driver of the Corvair stupid enough to try again, and Brody challenged him back, pumping the brakes suddenly as the kid was going to bump.

There, Brody thought with a grin, looking in the

rearview at the kid's shocked expression. That had scared the crap out of him well enough.

Then playtime was over, and Brody took advantage of his position, hitting the gas and rocketing toward the finish line.

There were boos and cheers, but he barely heard them, scanning the crowd at the sides for Hannah. He didn't see her anywhere.

Getting out, he took his money with barely a glance and left the car behind. Business was done, and he walked through the crowd, sought out Aiden. Still no sign of Hannah.

"That was stellar!"

Brody acknowledged his nephew, still distracted. Had he only imagined seeing Hannah?

"Thanks. These are your winnings. Give half to your friend for the use of his car, and extra to repair the dents from the bumping. The rest I'm going to hold on to so you can use it on the Mustang."

"Okay."

Brody was shocked at Aiden's easy agreement. Teenagers.

"Let's get out of here," Brody said.

He'd turned to walk back up to the car when he finally spotted Hannah. Taking pictures and completely oblivious to his presence. But not for long, he thought, heading in her direction, his nephew in tow.

7

HANNAH COULDN'T BELIEVE how cool this was. How could Brody have even considered leaving her behind when he knew she was looking for more adventure? Maybe he hadn't wanted her to know he was driving in an illegal drag race? The moment their eyes met through the lens of the camera, it was obvious that he was as shocked to see her as she was to see him behind the wheel of that car.

What was he thinking?

Still, she'd been as rapt as the rest of the crowd watching the two drivers race to the end of the strip, battling it out on the way back. Though she knew Brody was better than any driver they could set against him, she still worried when the cars were bumping and swerving around on the old, rutted road.

Her attention was diverted by all of the action and spectacle around her. She'd been worried about taking pictures at first, but no one seemed to care when she told them the pictures were for her blog. Some of the kids even posed by their cars.

She needed a better wide-angle lens—an item she

was going shopping for immediately, she decided. But for the first time since she'd started this photo blogging venture, she was actually taking pictures of something exciting.

"Hannah."

She whirled around, nearly dropping her camera when she found Brody glaring at her, a young man standing slightly behind him.

"Brody," she said in the same tone, lifting her camera to get a shot of him and the boy, who was clearly another driver. He was young and tough looking, sporting a black T-shirt with a racing emblem on the front and the words, Ask Forgiveness, Not Permission.

"How did you even know about this place?" Brody asked. "You shouldn't be here."

She arched an eyebrow, not feeling very apologetic. "Funny, I was thinking the same about you. You should be glad it was me taking that picture and not, oh, Marsha Zimmer."

"I was here to get *him*," Brody said, pointing a thumb behind him at the kid, who must be his nephew, Hannah realized. "The racing was… I didn't plan on it, but it was an unexpected situation. What's your excuse?"

Hannah looked at him as if he'd lost his mind, then turned to raise her camera to grab a few more shots before she responded, "I don't need an excuse. I don't need to ask permission *or* forgiveness, thank you very much."

The kid snorted, and Brody shot him a look.

Ticked off by Brody's domineering attitude, Hannah walked away without saying another word, intending to take some more pictures. A second later, Brody was right behind her, the kid hanging back.

"So that's your nephew?" she asked, sparing him a glance before she took a shot of two girls in stiletto heels both bent under the hood of a car, checking out the engine.

She'd spoken with them earlier and found out they owned and raced the car. In fact, they were one of the few all-female racing teams. Hannah had been fascinated by them and their story about how they'd gotten into racing. She didn't know their real names, of course, but she couldn't wait to write about them.

The girls joked that they changed into their boots or sneakers before they got in the car, but the "dome heels" and the short skirts threw the guys off. It made the pair seem less threatening, allowing them to get the drop on their competitors out on the track.

"Yes, and you know that's the reason I came here. I only ended up in that car... Hannah, could you put down the camera?" he said, sounding irritated.

She did as he asked, but didn't say one more word.

"I'm sorry I said what I did. I know I was out of line, I was just shocked to see you. How *did* you get here? And it *is* a dangerous place."

"I followed you after you blew me off and left the house. And I think I'm a lot safer taking pictures than you were driving," she said. "How'd that happen? You fell in a car and it took off?" She spared sarcasm in her tone.

"No. Aiden was scheduled to race, and I didn't want him to do it, but the stakes were already set. I tried to buy out his bet, but they wouldn't go for it. If he reneged, they'd have taken the car to make up for the losses—and to discourage people from backing out of other races. But the car doesn't belong to Aiden, so I took his place. I settled the bets and made sure he didn't lose the car or kill himself. I couldn't let him get in that car, and so I did it."

Hannah's irritation dissolved like sugar in rain.

"That was good of you, Brody. I'm sorry for being so snotty about it, but I thought you'd come to race, which is why you didn't want me with you."

It was his turn to look surprised. "What? No. I haven't done this kind of thing in over a decade," he said, shaking his head. But then his lips stretched into a happy smile. "But it was fun. Nice to show that little twerp in the Corvair a lesson, as well."

"How did you convince them to let you take Aiden's spot? They must have known you'd be a ringer."

"They didn't recognize me. Sometimes that happens when I'm not on the track. People don't really know me in plain clothes."

Hannah nodded. "This is amazing," she said in awe, looking over the field of bodies and cars. It painted a picture that was young and powerful, the music slamming a beat so strong she could feel it through the pavement along with the rumble of the engines.

"We should get out of here before all hell breaks loose, as it's likely to."

She looked around the scene, not as miffed as she was, but still reluctant to leave. This was what she wanted, what she craved, dangerous or not. The vibe here was raw, real and edgy. Brody sighed and slid a hand over her shoulder.

"Okay, listen, you're right. I should have let you

come with me. I should have known you'd appreciate an opportunity like this. Did you get good pictures?"

She smiled at him again, genuinely this time. "I got some incredible pictures."

"I can't wait to see them," he responded, looking to each side as if worried. Then a car skidded off the track, hitting a tree, flames lighting up that end of the runway.

Hannah gasped as the other car in the race skidded through the finish line, forcing onlookers back several feet at the last minute. She was also relieved to see someone exiting the flaming car, but then a fight broke out near the finish line. Things were turning ugly fast.

"Okay, let's go," she agreed.

"Where's your car?"

"Up the road a little. Yours?"

"Parked off to the side in a patch of trees."

Brody's attention perked as they heard sirens in the distance, and he picked up the pace.

"C'mon, we need to leave, or our first engagement picture will be mug shots," he said, only partly joking.

They made it to their cars and left quickly, Brody ahead of her with his nephew, just in time to see at least a dozen Florida Highway Patrol cars speed past them, heading toward the airstrip.

A tingle sped down Hannah's spine, making her shiver as she watched the lights in the rearview. She didn't want to get arrested, certainly, but the close call was exciting. She thought about all the ways she might work out that excitement once she got back to the farm and was alone with Brody. That set off a whole new set of shivers. Then her thoughts turned serious again.

He hadn't been out there racing for kicks, and his real reason for being there touched Hannah. Brody would clearly do anything for the people he cared about. He had even tried to protect her, though Hannah didn't want to be protected.

She was finally living, not simply observing or imagining, and it was wonderful. This was what she'd been missing all those years, hiding in her office behind sheets of numbers. She definitely needed to catch up.

On the side of the road Hannah noted a bar where the parking lot was crammed with motorcycles. She wondered if Brody might take her there, or if he rode a bike. She was fairly sure that if it had wheels, he'd probably mastered it.

Maybe she'd enjoy having a motorcycle, she mused. Women rode all the time these days, and it would save money on gas, too. There were so many possibilities. So much to explore.

She followed Brody through the dark, unfamiliar streets. He stopped in front of a small ranch-style home and signaled her to wait as he dropped the boy off.

It was a reminder that while they were going to be married, what they had now really wasn't much different from what they'd had during their month-long affair. She was still an outsider. Not really part of the family. Not really his wife in the truest sense.

Which was how she wanted it, right? The last thing she needed now was to be tied down. She was only starting to realize her independence and discover her own dreams.

He came back out shortly after, approaching her car and laying his arm on the roof, seemingly giant from her seated position.

"Sorry about that. I would have invited you in, but I figured Brandi wasn't going to be happy with Aiden, and I wanted to talk to her privately for a minute, try to help the kid out if I could."

He was a big man. Hannah loved how his shirt stretched across the muscles of his chest, and couldn't help admiring the carved lines of his biceps and forearms, so nicely shaped and strong. It made her swallow hard, licking her lips.

"I understand completely—no worries," she replied, her voice more breathless than she intended. She couldn't help herself from reaching up, touching his arm.

The move made him lean down, and she noticed, in the glow of the streetlight, how the pulse hammered in his throat from her simple touch.

"I'm starving," he said. "You?"

All she could do was nod.

Instead of going back to his own car, Brody crossed around to her passenger door, getting in.

"What about your car?"

"I'll get it tomorrow, or Brandi can drive it back over. I've spent enough time away from you tonight."

His tone was laced with such intention and emotion, it made her heart leap. Hannah had to focus sharply to keep her attention on the road as she pulled away from the curb.

Her task was made even more difficult when Brody's hand slipped down over her skin and under her shorts, stroking a tender spot.

"I won't be able to focus on my driving if you keep that up," she said on a shaky laugh, wanting him to continue but knowing it wasn't the best idea.

He smiled, but withdrew his hand. "So pull over. There's a spot up ahead, on the right."

Hannah saw it, a narrow road that veered off into trees. She followed it up a sharp hill, where a few seconds later they emerged out on a field that overlooked wetlands that stretched forever into the distance.

"Where are we?" she breathed. "This is gorgeous. It's magical, how the moon reflects on the water."

"It's the far end of Myakka River State Park," Brody said, but from his tone, she could tell that he wasn't interested in the view.

It was dark, quiet and private.

Hannah turned the car off, her senses taking over.

She'd never had sex in a car before. So many firsts in one day.

"These front seats aren't very comfortable," she said.

"My thought exactly."

Seconds later, they were in the back of her small car, making out like teenagers, and she was having the time of her life. Again.

Her earlier ideas about riding a motorcycle were forgotten. Hannah knew, as Brody eased her shorts down, that she was never, ever giving up this car.

BRODY HAD HAD more women in the backseats of cars than he could count. As one would expect, it was one of his favorite places to work off some steam, especially after a race.

But Hannah blew his mind. While she'd let him dominate at home in the shower, in the car, she took control, riding him with abandon until, her body racked with release, he'd banded his arms around her and gave in to the pleasure, as well.

It was fast, hot and incredible. He held her there for a long while as their breathing evened, not wanting the moment to pass. Tenderness that he'd never experienced for anyone else before overwhelmed him.

Hannah was so sweet, throwing herself completely into life, giving everything. She thought that she was boring or unadventurous, but of all the things Brody had experienced in life, none of it was as exciting as being with her like this.

Which made him crave more. He'd been around enough to know that it would probably wear off in time, but for now, she was exactly what he needed. And then some.

"Still hungry?" he asked against her ear.

"Absolutely."

"Vixen. I mean for food."

She laughed, and that made him happy. He wanted her happy.

"Oh, that. Yes."

"There's a twenty-four-hour diner back a mile or two from here, if that's good."

"Perfect."

They untangled their bodies in the cramped space, and fifteen minutes later, they were sliding into a booth.

He hadn't been to the place for years, but it hadn't

changed much. The red vinyl seats had been updated to newer, shinier red vinyl. Also updated were the tables, stools and counter. Otherwise, it was all the same, including the coin-fed jukeboxes at each table and the racing and other sports memorabilia all over the walls.

Brody got some change for a dollar at the register, and they had fun picking some songs—all of them at least a decade old—before ordering cheeseburgers and fries with milk shakes. It was a heavy midnight meal, but he was always starving after a race, and after sex.

He might as well be a teenager with his first date, he thought, looking at Hannah, her eyes bright. A very horny teenager.

Her color was still high from what had happened in the car, lips red from kissing. He reached over, taking her hand across the table.

"I suppose we should shop for a ring tomorrow," he said, studying her fingers, pale skin that was only slightly tanned from the Florida sun. He tried to imagine how a ring would look on her slim finger. His ring.

"What? Absolutely not. I can't let you do that."

"Why not? People will expect it, and it's not as though I can't afford it, Hannah."

He knew what she was thinking, though she didn't say it, her expression suddenly tense.

A ring made it feel more real. For him, too. But for some reason, it didn't cause him the anxiety it seemed to cause for her.

"A lot of people skip the traditional symbols these days," she countered. "Women keep their own names—which I will—and they don't wear rings or have big weddings," she continued.

"True, but I don't want the media, or my family, thinking I'm a cheapskate. Consider it a gift. A thank-you. For you to keep, to do whatever you want with later. Maybe it could finance a new adventure down the line," he added. He realized the mistake of his words as soon as they passed his lips.

She withdrew her hand.

"I'm sorry. I didn't mean it like that, obviously. It's not a payoff," he said in a rush, wishing he could erase what he'd said. "Not like that at all. It's difficult to…I don't know, make what we're doing—"

"Real and not real at the same time?" she offered.

"Yeah."

Their food arrived, and Brody was glad to not have to say anything while they ate and listened to music, which helped ease the tension between them.

After they finished eating, Brody broached the topic again, choosing his words more carefully this time.

"I want to do right by you, Hannah. Regardless of the details, I'll be your husband, and while it lasts I want it to be as real as it can be. How I feel about you, how you turn me on and everything else… I like being with you. You're a friend, and I hope you always will be, even…after we're not together anymore. So let me buy you a ring, because of that. Okay?"

She sipped her milk shake, drawing his attention to her mouth, which always caused his heart to stutter. What other woman had ever affected him like Hannah did?

As she put her cup down, she nodded, seeming to

agree. He wondered why she didn't say anything, but then noticed her eyes were bright with unshed tears.

Oh, crap, he'd made her cry, he thought in a panic, unsure what he'd done this time, but then she smiled. Brody was mute with confusion.

"Sorry, I don't mean to be so emotional, but that was so sweet. You're a good man, Brody. I care about you, too, and you definitely turn me on," she said, her cheeks flushing with her admission.

Sweet and bold were an intriguing mix in this woman. Brody was fascinated as he watched her emerge from her shell.

"Okay, then, that's settled. Ring shopping to-morrow. I really would like to see your pictures," he added, changing the subject. "Do you have to get them developed? Or do you do it yourself?"

"Digital. I took a course in developing film back in college, and I remember how, I think. For now, I'm going with digital, which is easier on the road. This way, I can get them on my computer and on the blog immediately."

"Smart thinking."

The door to the diner opened and a group of people came in, so loud they drowned out the music and all conversation. Brody glared, but then recognized the man who had been running the bets at the race. With him he had the same two thugs he'd had back at the airstrip. Brody was surprised they hadn't been arrested, but they must have had an escape route set up.

"We need to leave," he said quietly to Hannah.

Just then, the server who had been waiting on them approached the table with the bill and a shy smile.

"Here's your bill, but it's on the house. The owner,

all of us really, are huge racing fans. I wondered if you could sign this for me," she said, pulling a diner hat out of her apron pocket. "I was sorry to hear you retired. My husband, son and I are huge fans, Mr. Palmer."

Brody knew that he was caught and couldn't leave now.

"That's really nice of you, thank you," he said with a smile, taking the hat and a marker from her, signing it and then leaving a tip that was bigger than the bill.

He put his own hat back on, hoping no one else had noticed, but no such luck. The place was relatively empty and someone asking for an autograph was very visible. As was his picture on the far wall, he noted suddenly. His back had been to it before. As he noticed it, the server piped up again.

"If you could sign that, too, it would be awesome."

He smiled, trying to find a way out. "I live close by and could come back another time to do that, perhaps? It's late, and my date is tired," he explained with a wink.

"Of course. It would be great to have you come back," the young woman said with a wide smile.

A few other patrons noticed and approached the table, too, and Hannah watched in fascination, unaware that this was the last thing they needed at the moment. But Brody couldn't be rude to fans. It was another one of his few unbreakable rules. Hopefully, the guys across the diner wouldn't think much about it.

That ended up being another empty hope—they approached the table, too.

Brody met the gaze of the bookie, not backing down.

"Who the heck are you, old man? Some movie star

or something? You know, from silent film?" he said, getting a laugh from his buddies.

Brody flicked a glance in Hannah's direction. She tried not to appear too worried and probably failed.

"That's Brody Palmer, you nitwit," one of the other customers who had asked for his signature said with a sneer. "See the poster? If your generation ever got their faces out of their video games you might know a local celebrity when you saw one. Don't you follow racing?"

And that was that, Brody realized, pinching the bridge of his nose.

The punk leaned on the table. "A professional, huh? So you're a ringer? You took money from me, old man. And your boy did, too. That's cheating, and that's not a good thing."

Brody noticed one of the thugs eyeing Hannah in the wrong way, and he drew himself up to his full height, pulling their gazes back to him.

"Listen, fellas, I was helping out my nephew, like I said. I can give you your money back, with interest, no problem. But this is a nice place, with nice people. They don't need any trouble. Why don't we take this conversation outside?"

The bookie and the two guys with him were solid, but not too big. Brody figured he could take them if he needed to.

"Sure, we can go outside," the bookie said with a chuckle, stepping back. "Do this old school."

Brody turned to Hannah. "I'll be back in a minute."

Her eyes widened and she shook her head, but he was already walking to the door. This wasn't going to help his reputation any, but he didn't see that he had much choice. At least outside, no one else would get hurt.

Except that Hannah was following.

He turned to tell her not to follow when he saw one of the thugs on the side of the bookie draw back and level his fist at Brody's face. Hannah lurched to warn him and was yanked away by the other guy.

Brody saw red at anyone touching her, especially so roughly. Ducking the punch and sending his attacker into a table, he turned to deal with the guy who was still holding on to Hannah.

Brody stepped forward, and the bookie interfered with his progress.

"You'd better back off," he said to Brody, and pulled a knife from his pocket.

A very nasty-looking knife.

Brody put his hands up. "Just let my girl go and we're good."

"No, we're not good. But maybe now we're in a better bargaining position," the guy said with a slimy smile. "I think you need to pay up more than you did, all things considered. You cheated, and you hurt one of my guys."

Brody saw the fans who had talked with him earlier take a few steps forward to help, but he gave them a look that he hoped stopped any well-intentioned rescues. If this guy had a knife, the other one might have one, too. Brody couldn't risk anything happening to Hannah.

"Fine, I'll write you a check. Name it, but let her go."

Suddenly Brody looked up to see Hannah break free. She let out some kind of growl, a feral, infuriated noise as she swung the camera by its strap and hit the bookie hard enough to send him flying forward into the nearest table, his knife flying in the opposite direction.

Brody jumped in and lunged to get the knife as he saw the thug who had held Hannah reach for her again.

That was two times too many that the jerk had put his hands on her, and it was Brody's turn to get angry. He closed the space between them quickly and dropped the jerk with one punch, out cold.

Applause rose on the other side of the diner, and Brody looked up to see his fans had the bookie cornered at a table, and they were smiling approvingly.

Brody looked for Hannah to make sure she was okay and saw her sitting on the floor, staring at the pieces of her camera. There were many pieces, and it didn't look as though it could be put back together again.

"Oh, honey, I'm so sorry," Brody said, squatting down and helping her pick up the busted camera.

"It's okay. I still have the SD card with the pictures," she said, raising her face to his. He expected her to be upset, perhaps in tears, at losing one of her prized possessions, but instead, that feral gleam still shone in her eyes as she switched her gaze to the bookie. "It was *so* worth it."

Brody wasn't sure he'd ever wanted to kiss her more. So he did.

8

HANNAH FOUND BRODY frowning as he sat with a news-paper and coffee the next morning.

"Morning," she said, taking one of his hands in hers and inspecting the bruises from the punch he'd landed the night before. "Hurt?"

"Not much. I've had worse."

Without elaborating, he turned the paper toward her, and she gaped at the headline. Has Bad Boy Brody Palmer Finally Found His Perfect Bad Girl?

"Oh, no…"

The picture was pretty good, actually, catching the instant Hannah hit the bookie with her camera, and Brody pulling his fist back to hit the guy who was reaching to grab her.

"Look at our faces… We look as though we're going to kill people," she said, holding her hand to her face, smothering a laugh.

Brody's eyebrows rose. "You think that's funny?"

She tried to repress her smile, but it was hard. "Well, yeah."

Her eyes scanned the brief article below, citing

the pictures were taken from a fan's phone; there was also a phone video available online. It featured the bookie saying that Brody had cheated in an illegal street race earlier in the evening, which had started the entire incident.

"Oh…no," Hannah said again.

"Yeah, that cat's out of the bag, and then some. I already heard from Jud this morning—he's the lead publicist with my sponsor—and he didn't know whether to be angry that I was in a fight, or happy that I was getting engaged," Brody said, shaking his head. "He suggested that I might want to find someone less likely to get into public brawls," he added.

"What did you say to that?"

"I told him I'd rather have a woman who can hold her own in a fight."

Hannah's grin twitched again, and Brody couldn't help but laugh, too.

"I thought this was about making me look better, not making you look worse, my love," he joked.

Hannah choked on her laughter at his endearment. Of course he meant it jokingly, as he hadn't seemed to think twice about it, but the words had struck her straight in the heart. She turned to the coffeepot to pour a cup and get hold of herself, surprised to find her hands shaking.

She was still tired, and adrenaline had hit her as soon as she saw the paper; that was all, she reassured herself.

"So we probably should go out for a ring after breakfast."

Hannah was riding an emotional roller coaster of enormous proportions, and it was making her dizzy.

The police had shown up to arrest the bookie and his friends—everything witnessed and attested to by Brody's fans, so they weren't detained at all, thank goodness. After returning home, they'd both been charged up and worked off that energy in the most delightful ways, until they'd fallen asleep.

Hannah had woken up wondering how this could be her life. Street races, amazing sex, even midnight brawls with bad guys…and she was getting married.

The newspaper on the table made it official.

"Hey, are you okay?"

Brody took the pot she was still holding—lost in thought—from her hands, putting it on the counter. He pulled her against him, his arms coming around her.

"Yeah, I am, I'm just… It's a lot to process. I guess I'll get used to it."

"I know you will."

He wrapped her up tight against him, snug and safe, anxiety and confusion melting away like it always did. Being close to Brody was the only time things seemed right. Normal.

It was when her thoughts and emotions weren't muddled by sex or how perfect he felt next to her that things got a little dicey.

"I was thinking…" she said, facing him. "Maybe instead of a ring, we could go camera shopping? Mine is toast."

Brody nodded. "We have time to do both. We don't have to be at my parents' house until seven."

"No, I mean, um, instead of a ring."

"What? Why?"

Hannah shrugged. "I'll certainly get more use out

of it," she offered with a hopeful smile. "And I never was much for jewelry."

Hannah couldn't go through with letting Brody buy her a ring. It wasn't…right. A camera was much less fraught with complications.

"I don't know about that," he said, not conceding as easily as she'd like.

Hannah bit her lip, trying to keep her tone light. "How about I buy my own camera—it's a business expense after all—and then we find wedding rings we like and split the cost? But no diamond. Just the bands."

It occurred to her that this had to be the most unromantic discussion of engagement and wedding rings that ever occurred in the history of the world, but Hannah held her line.

"Can I ask why you changed your mind about a ring? You agreed last night."

"I know it's probably silly, but I need to hold on to some of the dream, you know? If I ever get married—for real—I want to have the whole enchilada. The romantic proposal, the ring, and have it be perfect. I want that ring to be on my hand forever. This one won't be."

Hannah had a deep need to protect that dream; it still meant something.

"Okay, we can do that," he said. He didn't look entirely happy about it, but he agreed. "Except that we're not splitting the cost on rings. And I get to buy you the camera."

"Brody—"

"Don't argue. You did lose yours to keep me from

getting knifed, after all, and this marriage was my crazy idea."

Hannah looked away, frowning at the sharp stab of...something...that his phrasing caused. She knew what he meant, so why was it bothering her so much? It *was* crazy—that was precisely why she was going along with it.

"Okay, you win, but any other wedding expenses we split, so let's keep them small," she said brightly, putting her game face on.

She expected him to be happy to have won the debate, but he didn't look it.

"Hannah, what's going on?" he asked.

"What do you mean?"

"I can see how tense you are. Something's bothering you."

She took a deep breath. Brody wasn't like the typical men she often heard women talking about, the ones who weren't attentive or perceptive. He saw too much. Or she didn't hide her feelings well enough. Or both.

But she couldn't exactly tell him that...what? She was afraid she might be feeling more for him than she should? That it hurt whenever she was reminded that their marriage wasn't going to be the real thing? At least not in the forever sense?

She pulled herself up and met his concerned look, giving him the most honest answer she could. "I need to remember that this is an adventure. For it to be fun. I don't want to dwell on the complications, but I'm not used to being so impulsive, like you are. I'm still figuring out how to handle it all."

It was the truth, but vague enough that she didn't

humiliate herself by saying that she had to keep her
heart protected, or that she had to remind herself not
to believe what they had was genuine. Not with him.
Brody could turn her inside out if she let that happen. He'd been completely honest with her, and she
was the one who had told the reporter that she was
his fiancée. So she'd gotten herself into this, really.

Still, it would be all too easy to want this to be real.
Really, 100 percent real.

"Hannah, if you don't want to go through with this,
I understand. If you have doubts or worries, that's
okay."

"No. I want to do it. We're in it now and, hey, like
the paper says, we're meant for each other—both of
us are bad apples," she joked.

If she was going to try to change—to really change
and live more adventurously, she had to stop second-
guessing everything, and throw herself in. "So let's
be bad together."

He smiled. "I think that sounds good."

"I need to frame that headline, I think."

"That's a great idea," he said with a grin, dipping in
for a kiss, and then another. "Let's be bad right now."

The kiss got hotter, and all of her worries were
erased by the scorching blur of arousal. Would it always be like this? she wondered as Brody stroked her
concerns away. Or would their attraction cool, making it easier to leave later?

Stop thinking, her body demanded.

"We have to get ready to go shopping," she murmured as his lips did delicious things to the nerve
endings along her shoulder.

Brody chuckled. "Really? Shopping? Now?"

As much as she wanted to continue what they'd started, Hannah also needed to know she could maintain some sense of self-control.

"I really need that camera," she said.

He drew back, looking at her in astonishment until bubbles of laughter broke through her facade and infected him, as well. She loved his laugh, and she loved laughing with him.

He stepped back and then scooped her up, making her shriek in surprise.

"What are you doing?"

"We're going shopping, but we need a shower first, don't you think?"

Hannah sighed. She couldn't argue with that.

BRODY HELPED HIS mother pull heavy dishes out of the oven—she'd invited them over instead of everyone meeting at a restaurant. He was thankful, given that the media had been dogging him all day while they'd been out shopping. Somehow they'd gotten Hannah's phone number, too, and they'd both had to shut their phones off. Brody's sponsor was thrilled—Brody was less so.

"Hannah seems like a nice young woman," his mother said casually as she took the foil off a large pan of fried chicken. She'd made enough food for an army, as usual. "Though I couldn't help but notice that she wasn't wearing a ring."

His mom's blue eyes met his over the wide surface of the granite island, and Brody shrugged, wanting to tell the truth as much as he could.

"We both agreed to only wearing wedding bands."

"This was all so fast, Brody, so tell me, before I

read it in the paper, am I going to be a grandmother? Not that I mind, but—"

"No! Absolutely not. Come on, Mom," Brody said, cursing as he picked up a hot casserole without grabbing a pot holder first, then apologizing to his mom for his language.

"Well, what is someone to think? You never said a word, never mentioned Hannah and we've never met her. Now suddenly you're getting married—and in a matter of days. It seemed logical to think there was a reason, and your father and I are fine with it. We're quite progressive, as you know, and—"

Brody crossed to his mother and put a hand on either of her small shoulders, looking her in the eye.

"Mom, Hannah isn't pregnant. I promise. We just…reconnected after having been together before, last year. This time, it was…right."

Brody turned to the task he was helping with, afraid his mother might see too much.

Because being with Hannah did feel right. Very right.

When she'd refused a ring because she wanted her first engagement ring to be her only one, to have a real proposal and a future with the man who offered it to her, the thought had gutted him.

Another man putting his ring on Hannah's finger, another man promising her forever. Another man in her bed, and her having his children.

"Honey, are you okay?"

"What? Yeah, sorry, Mom. I can't believe you made so much food. Who else did you invite, the fifth battalion?"

His mother laughed at his diversion, which was

good, because Brody didn't really want to follow his previous train of thought. What he had with Hannah was good, and he enjoyed it—as far as it went. But their future paths were different. He'd go back to racing, and she'd go off on her own adventures.

He refused to overthink it.

"No, it's just the six of us, but you know Aiden eats like a typical teenage boy, which means he'll consume enough for three."

"Brandi and Aiden will be here?"

"Of course. They want to celebrate your news, too."

Brody nodded, holding the pan of chicken and the door for his mom as she passed in front of him out to the dining room.

The beachside condo was where his parents had moved after selling their larger home, but his mother had a talent for making any space cozy. The dining room table could hold only the six of them, but the room provided a view of the gulf through French doors. A gorgeous sunset simmered low over the water, casting purple-and-orange light everywhere.

"You can't beat that view," he commented, hearing his father chatting with Hannah in the other room, and her laughter floating back. What were they talking about?

"We enjoy it every single day. The ones from the bedrooms are equally nice, and to be able to walk out onto the beach? It's heaven. Of course, it's all because of you, my dear," his mom said with a smile, squeezing his arm and kissing his cheek before she returned to the kitchen.

He knew she meant because he'd made the down

payment his anniversary gift to them, and he knew the previous owner of the condo, who'd given him a deal.

That his parents were happy meant everything to Brody. They'd always been there for him, and he never forgot that.

Because of that, lying to them about anything made him feel sick. He was lucky she'd gone back to the kitchen and that Brandi and Aiden's voices filled the front entry as they arrived, or he might have spilled everything to his mom right then and there.

Everyone came in then, Aiden looking as if nothing had happened the night before as he leaned over the table rubbing his hands together at the sight of the fried chicken. Brandi followed, but she didn't look as happy as her son, completely ignoring the food. In fact, she looked ticked, and made a beeline directly for Brody.

Great.

"*What* is going on?" she asked Brody as she pulled him over to the French doors.

"Listen, I would have told you, but we only just decided that we wanted to—"

"I don't mean about your engagement. I want to know why you think you had the right to promise Aiden that you'll help him get his license and take him to the track? Teach him to drive? Are you out of your mind?"

Brody took a breath, but he was somewhat relieved she wasn't asking about him and Hannah.

"Brandi, it's the safest option. Let me teach him, work on the car with him over at the farm, and that will keep him out of street racing. That's the deal I made with him. He will get himself killed if you insist on controlling him. What he was doing out there last night was a lot riskier than anything he'll do with me."

"How so? You're teaching him to race. You're feeding that need in him, and I won't have it," she said, her entire body vibrating with tension.

Brody glanced out at the shimmering water, then back at his sister. He could only imagine what she'd lost when Aiden's father had died, and he knew how difficult it had been for her. And he hadn't been around nearly as much as he should have been to help. Not for her, or for Aiden. So he was going to help now, but he could see the fear in her eyes. Somehow, he had to convince her to let it go.

"Believe me, Bran, that need is part of him. It's his father in him, and it won't go away. Let me help him do it right."

She shook her head. "I don't want him racing *at all*. I want him to go to college, to find something else—"

"You can't make those choices for him. It's painful, but you can't. Let me teach him, maybe get it out of his system, and who knows what will happen in a few years? Maybe he'll decide it's not for him."

Brody didn't believe that; he saw the fire in the kid. It had been in his father and in Brody himself. He had to get Brandi to see reason.

"That's another thing. You're giving him a car?"

"No. It's Marco's old car, and it's been at the farm for almost two decades. It's a rust bucket now, and it will take at least two years for us to fix it up, so he won't get it until he's over eighteen anyway. But he's going to have to learn to be patient and to earn it. I promise."

Brandi's eyes glistened with tears as she stared

at the water, but she didn't shed them as she met his gaze again.

"You think this will keep him off the streets?"

"I do. It's the deal I made, and I'll make sure he sticks to it."

"Okay. I still don't like it, but I know you're right. He'll get himself arrested or worse in these illegal races, so if you can stop that, then I'll go along with it. Maybe throw some better math grades in the deal, as well," she said with a smirk.

Then she hugged him.

"It's good to have you here now, Brody. Aiden needs you, and I do, too. I guess I should say congratulations," she continued, kissing his cheek. "And for what it's worth, I met Hannah briefly at the house and I liked her. I think you're going to be okay."

He watched her leave, glad to have settled the issue, but feeling more and more pressure of his own making. So many promises to keep—to his family, to his sponsors and to himself. Somehow he had to make it all work, though in his heart, he had no idea how the heck he was going to pull that off. Brody looked out at the diminishing sun, feeling as though he was sinking with it.

9

HANNAH WAS UP EARLY—surprising, given that she and Brody had made love long into the night again. They couldn't get enough of each other. As if they were real newlyweds, or almost newlyweds, unable to come up for air.

She'd enjoyed his family, finding them as charming as their son was. They'd welcomed her warmly, though with a certain amount of curiosity, of course. Hannah almost wished they had been less friendly so she wouldn't have liked them so much so quickly, but that was impossible. They'd made her feel like part of the family right off.

But she'd decided before she fell asleep that she was going to stop worrying about all of it. It would work itself out, and in the meantime, she would enjoy this gambit instead of constantly undermining it with doubts and worries.

At the moment, she fussed around the big kitchen, making breakfast and smiling as she searched for some of the fresh oranges she'd seen in the fridge. She'd make some juice while the eggs and bacon sizzled on the stovetop. Brody had still been snoring when she'd left him in bed, and she wanted to surprise him.

As the juicer whirred, she plated the eggs and bacon, grabbed toast from the toaster and arranged it all on a tray she'd found in the pantry. A carafe of coffee completed the arrangement.

Satisfied with the result, she picked up the tray and headed for the stairs.

She'd never served breakfast in bed to a man before. It was fun, she thought as she crept up the stairs, carefully balancing the tray.

Thinking about the night they'd shared made her smile softly. He'd been attentive and sweet, and as tender as he'd been passionate.

She paused in front of the door, realizing she had a problem. Both hands full, she had no way to open the door and deliver her lovely breakfast. Frustrated, she turned to go back down the hall and rest the tray on a small table near the wall when the bedroom door opened, revealing a sleepy, rumpled Brody wearing only a sheet hitched around his waist.

Hannah nearly fumbled the tray and lost it completely, but he reached out a hand and stabilized it for her.

"I wondered where you were… What's this?"

"Breakfast," she announced, foolishly nervous. Would he think it was silly? Too domestic? "I was up early, and I thought I'd surprise you, but then I got stuck at the door."

He looked at the full tray and smiled.

"No one's ever done this for me before."

"Really?" Hannah was so happy to be his first

in anything that she couldn't contain her pleasure. "Maybe you could go crawl back in bed and pretend to be surprised all over again."

"I have a better idea," he said, slipping both hands around the edges of the tray. "You go get back in bed, and I'll bring this in for both of us."

She smiled and handed the tray over. "Okay, thanks. That was getting heavy," she admitted.

She crossed the room, kicking off her slippers to get back into the huge, luxurious bed that took up a good deal of the room, with a quilted headboard and piles of comfortable pillows and blankets. The colors were masculine, though—the walls a basic neutral that emphasized the dark wood trim and hardwood floor. Decorative rugs were nice accents on the cool, bare wood floors, and Hannah was very comfortable in the space.

But then she spied the small table and chairs by the window, and crossed to the table, pulling the curtains apart and letting the sun stream inside.

"Let's eat here instead?"

"Sure," he agreed, carrying the tray to the table and setting it down. "This looks wonderful. Thank you."

"It's nice to have a fancy breakfast. Usually I grab coffee and go in the morning."

They took plates and she poured orange juice while he filled coffee cups, as routine as if they had been doing it for years. Like an actual couple.

"You like to cook?" he asked.

"I like to think about it," she said with a rueful laugh. "I watch cooking shows, collect cookbooks, but I rarely have the chance. I used to cook for my mother when I lived with her, and sometimes I make dinner for Reece and Abby, but mostly, when it's only me, I get takeout or have a salad."

"Seems to me you have natural talent for it—these are the best eggs I've ever had," he said appreciatively.

Hannah beamed at the compliment. The eggs *were* good.

"The secret is to use enough butter—if there's one thing you learn from reading French cookbooks, it's don't be afraid of butter. I added some seasoning salt and chives."

"They're delicious. Have you been to France?"

"I wish. Maybe someday. Reece and Abby have invited me a few times, but I haven't been able to get away because of work. I blew my vacation time last year on Daytona," she said with a smile. "I don't regret that one bit, of course. I guess work won't be a problem now. Maybe I'll plan to go next winter."

"You should. You can take cooking classes in Paris, you know."

"I've seen that in the travel brochures. You've probably gone for racing?"

He shook his head. "Not with the stock circuit, but I went over when Reece was racing a few times. I was there the day he had his accident. That was a tough one," he said, his mouth turning downward at the memory as he bit into his toast.

"I can only imagine," she said softly, reaching over to squeeze his hand. "You've been friends for a long time?"

She realized that while she knew both men, Reece for longer, of course, she didn't know about his friendship with Brody.

"Ever since we were working our way through the

ranks. Reece started out in the stock-car circuit here, but one trip to Europe and he was hooked on the road courses and never looked back."

"Not you?"

He shook his head, grabbing a napkin and pushing his empty plate back as he took his coffee and glanced out the window.

"Nope. It's always been about American muscle for me."

Hannah bit her lip, unsure if she should pry, but spoke anyway. "You miss it."

"I do. Or, I miss…things about it. I miss the driving and the cars. I miss the speed. I liked my team. But I don't miss…the spectacle, I guess. The media lately has reminded me of that. Constant interviews, constant posturing. It was all…a show. Honestly, that part, and the commercialism, the pressure from the sponsors, really started eating away at the fun."

Hannah was surprised. She'd thought he loved that part of it. The attention and the publicity.

"I never would have guessed that," she said, trying to put the pieces together, the different sides of the man sitting across from her. "You always seemed to eat it up. Or at least you were easy with it."

He smiled. "I don't mind it, but when it becomes too much about advertising, sponsors, money… something basic is lost. The love of it, I guess."

"Then why go back?"

"I guess I'd rather go out on my own terms when I do. And I still love it, the driving. I don't feel ready to leave yet. It's all I've ever known."

Hannah nodded. She could see it in his face, the love he felt for the sport, and some part of her was jealous. Driving owned a part of Brody that no one else would ever touch, not even her. She was about to ask him more when they were distracted by the sound of tires on the gravel of the front driveway.

Brody groaned, standing up quickly. "I completely forgot about this, sorry."

She looked down to see three cars pull in.

"Who are they?"

"They?" Brody said, looking back with a frown as he crossed to the window. "What the… It's supposed to be Aiden, coming over for a driving lesson and to work on the car for a bit. Looks as though he brought friends."

"Maybe he wants to show his famous uncle off," she said with a smile. "It's a good thing that you're doing there."

"I should make them get the horses out and clean the stalls first," Brody said with an evil grin that made Hannah laugh. "Could you take care of Zip? I can get the others after I'm done with the guys."

"I'm flattered that you trust me with him. He does flirt a lot," she teased.

"He does, but I trust you with everything. You should know that."

Hannah flushed with pleasure.

"I have to do more work on the blog," she said, excited to get on with it. "I put up some pictures from the race the other night and it got a huge response. So many comments, I almost couldn't believe it. And I had an email last night from a driving magazine asking if I could send them some more pictures, of the female racing pair, particularly."

"That's amazing! Congratulations."

Brody's excitement warmed her. He crossed the room to deliver a hot kiss to her lips. "You're going places, I know it. I'm happy for you. We can celebrate later," he added, wiggling his eyebrows.

He kissed her again before heading down to meet the boys, and Hannah pulled on her clothes, too. There was no point in taking a shower until after she took care of Zip.

Hannah's mind refocused on what else she could shoot that would keep the momentum on her blog going, and she also had to find some shots she thought the racing publication might take.

If they took the pictures, it would be her first real, professional sale.

The lucky break had reoriented her on her goals, and she smiled as she went downstairs, hearing the sound of engines roaring out front. Even though it was only the boys and their cars, the sound was becoming one that made her heart beat a little faster. It made her think of the track, racing and, most of all, Brody. He'd told her that racing got under your skin, in your blood, and she was starting to believe it. Or maybe it was the man.

She was trying to deny it, that maybe he was working his way into her heart. Maybe admitting it, if only to herself, would help her keep it under control.

She grabbed the new camera that Brody had insisted on buying her the afternoon before, one that was five times more expensive than what she would have bought for herself. He'd insisted, and she had to admit, she loved it. It had so many great features; she couldn't wait to get started.

Hannah planned to take some pictures of the

horses, and if they came out well, she'd have some framed for the house. Maybe one of Zip in particular, since she knew Brody had a soft spot for him.

As she walked down the porch steps, however, she couldn't help but notice Brody standing in the sun by the cars, all of the hoods raised, the four boys standing around him listening as if their lives depended on it. Something about it, how the men all grouped together, intense and oblivious to her presence, studying the open maws of the cars' engines, made her pause.

Adjusting some of the settings on her camera, she took some experimental shots, and then, excited about the sharp focus in the close-ups, continued. She clicked one of Brody slapping Aiden on the back, laughing, and one of a young man getting behind the wheel, looking intense as Brody leaned in, giving him instructions.

Mostly, she focused on Brody, very closely, for several more shots, her heart beating almost as quickly as the camera cycled through frame after frame as she studied his features in detail. He was so handsome, she almost couldn't put the camera down.

Several minutes passed when she realized she had almost completely forgotten about Zip, and reluctantly stopped taking pictures, heading down to the barn.

Zip was definitely happy to see her, as were the others. They put up with her taking a few pictures of them, heads hanging eagerly over the stalls, waiting for their breakfast. Eventually, they started making impatient noises, shuffling around their spaces, ready to get out into the sunshine.

She fed them all as she soaked up the relaxing presence of the animals. When they were done, she took

Zip, putting on his lead rope and walking him out into the sun. He went along with her, happy as they made their way to the corral.

Inside the corral, she walked with him, petting his sleek coat as the sun beat down, and wondered if the horse's good nature extended to letting her ride him. She rode bareback all the time and had since she was a kid. In fact, her father had once had a horse that resisted the saddle routinely and would only allow a rider on without one. Brody said Zip had also resisted the saddle from day one.

"Want to give it a try, Zip?" she said.

The horse stood still, as if waiting, and she took that as a good sign. Seconds later, she was up, and enjoying riding him in a light canter around the corral. He went along unperturbed, and Hannah offered him copious compliments as he did so.

"Good job, Zip. Maybe we'll try that again tomorrow."

But it was getting hot, and she didn't want to overwork him. She tugged him to a stop, about to dismount when a loud bang came from up the hill in the driveway, and Zip neighed loudly in fear, rearing back.

Hannah held on for dear life, trying to get the horse to calm down and to get her arms more firmly around his neck, but she couldn't hold on the second time he reared up, sending her flying off his back as he took off down the field.

BRODY ADJUSTED THE manifold under the hood of the Honda that Aiden's friend Rudy drove. Apparently Aiden had told some of his friends about his deal with

Brody, and he'd invited them along. Brody saw it as an opportunity and made the same deal with them: that he'd show them some of the ropes if they stayed out of street racing—and that meant taking any enhancements, like nitrous, out of their cars, period.

He quickly discovered that none of these guys really knew how engines worked, and if they didn't know how their cars worked, they couldn't drive them optimally.

So the first thing they did was to get a lesson on mechanics.

Rudy's car backfired when he started it and gunned the engine, and then again as he tried to adjust the timing and the fuel injection.

Brody heard Aiden swear, and he looked up to follow Aiden's gaze down the hill toward the corral in time to see Zip charging away and Hannah lying on the ground.

Heart twisting, Brody forgot what he was doing and ran to the corral, nearly turning his ankle in a rut, stumbling but pushing onward. By the time he got to the corral and through the gate, Hannah was brushing herself off, unaware he was there.

He reached her, pulling her around, searching her face, her body, for injury.

"What were you doing up on that horse? You could have been hurt, or worse. Are you okay? Does anything hurt?"

Hannah blinked, as if she couldn't quite understand him, and he studied her more intently.

"Did you hit your head?"

"No, I don't think so," she said, taking a breath.

"Just knocked the wind out of me, and I might have bruised my backside, but that's it."

"We should get you to the ER, just in case."

"Brody, I'm fine. That's not the first time I've fallen off a horse, you know," she said, pushing her hair back from her face.

"You didn't fall, you were thrown." He glared toward Zip. "That horse has to go."

Hannah put a hand on his, and shook her head. "No, he doesn't. He was fine, and we had a very nice ride. In fact, he was perfect until that engine noise scared him. It could have happened to any horse."

"Why were you up on him? And without any tack?"

She shrugged, stepping back and brushing more dirt from her jeans and shirt. "You said he was fighting the tack, so I thought I'd try riding him bareback. He liked it. Had no problem whatsoever, and wouldn't have thrown me if it weren't for the noise."

She was calm, practical Hannah, and Brody's heart started to beat at a more normal pace. He must still have looked worried, though, as she put her hands on either side of his face, as if *she* were concerned about *him*.

"I'm fine, Brody. Seriously."

Brody hauled her against him, running his hands over her back, as if to make sure she was telling the truth.

"You scared the daylights out of me. If anything had happened to you, I... I shouldn't have asked you to take care of him."

She scoffed and stepped back, out of his embrace. "I was happy to."

They looked at the horse eyeing them from the other side of the field, and Hannah suddenly lifted her hands to her mouth, letting go a loud whistle that nearly deafened Brody at such close proximity.

But he was astounded when Zip sauntered toward them, stopping by Hannah's side, nudging her with his head.

"I know, boy. It wasn't your fault," she said, kissing the horse on the bridge of his nose.

Then she did something even more incredible and pulled herself onto Zip's bare back.

"I don't want him having any negative associations from that ride, so I'm going to walk him around a few times, okay?" she asked Brody, though she wasn't really asking.

Brody watched as they moved away from him, Zip walking along calmly. He shot a glance up toward the house, making a sign to Aiden to make sure all engines were cut. There was nothing but silence as Brody watched Hannah ride the horse as if they were made of the same blood and bone.

Maybe Zip related to the calmness in her, the inner stability that was always part of the woman herself. Something Brody had gravitated to when he'd first met her, and something that didn't shift, even when she seemed less than sure of herself.

Stepping out of the corral, Brody saw her camera hanging on the post near the barn and grabbed it. He wasn't a professional, but he'd listened to the saleswoman in the shop, and he could take a picture. Something about this moment made him want to capture it, and he lifted the lens, which was already set for a close-up.

Clicking the pictures, his heart seemed to swell as he stared at Hannah, her hand stroking the horse's mane as she rode, her beautiful lips moving as she spoke to Zip, secrets between the two of them.

It was the happiest he'd ever seen Zip, who appeared ready and willing to ride all day if it was for Hannah.

Brody lowered the camera as Hannah dismounted and left the corral, her entire face glowing with happiness. Brody was almost jealous of the horse for a second, unsure if he'd ever made her quite that happy.

"He's so wonderful, Brody, did you see? I love him so much," she said.

But her eyes were on his, her smile for him, and the words made his heart stutter. Maybe because he wished they were for him, and not for the horse? The next thing he knew he was kissing her and she was clinging to him. Having her in his arms was all he cared about.

When he'd realized she'd fallen, his heart had stopped for a beat. All that had mattered to him in that moment—more than his family, his career, anything—was that Hannah could be injured.

Touching her now, with an inkling of what it would be like if he lost her or was never able to touch her again, he couldn't stop.

"Brody," she gasped, her eyes blurry with desire as she pushed back, putting some distance between them.

Brody didn't want distance, and pulled her back next to him, needing to reassure himself she was okay.

Finally, catcalls and beeping horns cut through the haze of his need, and he broke off the kiss.

When Brody glanced up the hill at his nephew and his friends, they broke out into applause, giving him a hearty thumbs-up.

He'd entirely forgotten they were there. That was what Hannah did to him. She made him forget everything.

Hannah's smile widened, even as her cheeks burned bright red. Brody swore under his breath, but laughed, too, their passion fading in the humor of the kids' response.

"Okay, I guess I'm not being the best role model here," he said, stepping away.

"Oh, I think you just became their absolute hero," Hannah said with an embarrassed chuckle. "I should finish the horses and let you get back to them."

"No, I'll help you. They've had enough for this morning, anyway, and I wouldn't mind finishing what we started once we get the horses out in the pasture."

Her lips parted and her eyes told him she'd like that, too. He waved to the guys and they waved back, getting the message. They got into their cars and drove off.

Inside the barn, Brody took the time to process his feelings and his reaction to Hannah almost being hurt. He'd completely freaked out, which was something he almost never did. Ever.

He cared for Hannah, of course. He always had. He enjoyed their time together, and he did trust her. Like a good friend. And a lover. The physical chemistry between them was explosive, but what they had was temporary. It wasn't love.

Loving someone wasn't a temporary situation, and it was one he couldn't allow himself to fall into. He would go back to racing next season, and she'd move on with her own life. They'd get a divorce at some convenient time, and that would be that.

He recited that to himself a few times and started to feel steadier. He'd panicked, understandable given his recent experience being thrown by Zip. He still shook his head at how casual she'd been about it, and how she'd climbed back up on the beast, more concerned about the horse's reaction than her own.

He admired that, and he admired Hannah. But he had to be clear about his own feelings. Admiration, sex and even caring were not love. Love wasn't part of the bargain, and they both knew that.

By the time they got the stables clean and returned to the house, hand in hand, Brody had almost convinced himself it was true.

10

ALMOST A WEEK after Zip had thrown her, most of the media attention about their engagement had lessened, and there had been no more brawls or other disasters. She and Brody had more or less settled into a nice rhythm with her work and his helping his teenage crew with their cars. Her days were spent wedding planning and working on her blog and her photos, and her nights were spent in passionate delirium with Brody.

Life was good.

The wedding was set now for Saturday, in four days, on the beach at Brody's parents' house. They had insisted on it, not wanting their son to get married in a courthouse. She couldn't say no to that generous offer, nor to Mrs. Palmer's and Brandi's offers of help, but Hannah kept it all manageable.

Her mother was coming into town in a day or so, and had made Hannah wait to shop for a dress. Reece hadn't been able to make it home from France, regrettably, and Abby had to mind the winery, so Hannah's best friends would not be at the wedding. She comforted herself with knowing that someday, when she got married for love, it would all be very different.

It was becoming more like a real wedding—which was necessary, of course, if the public and Brody's sponsors were to believe it—and she was trying to not let that get to her, focusing on her work as a distraction.

Yet the wedding and all of the fuss around it couldn't be further from her mind. She was at the local raceway with her camera, snapping shots of Brody with his group of students, which now had two more pupils.

She'd sent off pictures to a few other magazines that she had queried, and they were delighted to look at her work—especially when it included Brody Palmer.

Having a famous subject for her first published photos was certainly a leg up, but then, as Brody reminded her, he was benefitting from it, as well. He'd finally found a way to contribute that he really felt invested in. Helping these kids drive more safely and become more responsible about their choices was clearly important to him. And he made each and every one of them promise to stop racing illegally.

So far, so good.

Hannah knew that several of the boys—and one teenage girl, she was pleased to see—like Aiden, didn't have two parents, usually missing their father for various reasons. In that sense, Brody was more than a driving instructor. He was a role model who was showing them what a man could be. A good man.

Hannah wanted that message to be clear, so she made a deal with the most recent editor of a well-known sports publication to write a short article to go with her pictures, discussing this very issue. She wanted to talk more to Brody's students as well, and perhaps to other kids who were racing illegally. To find out why they chased the rush, took the risks. To reveal the kids as people, not just hoodlums, as they were often portrayed in the press.

Brody was impressed with a few of the teens and thought one or two, including Aiden, could even make it professionally if they kept at it. He didn't tell them that, not yet, so it didn't go to their heads, but she knew he was already setting up meetings with other professional drivers to come talk to the group. Everyone's excitement was high.

Hannah spent a lot of time studying Brody through her lens, as well. He was very photogenic—no surprise there—but even in a group of people, in a public place, through the lens, the world narrowed down to just the two of them.

They'd been there for hours, though, and she looked at her watch, wondering when they would be heading back to the ranch. She had more work to do, and she always looked forward to that time at the end of the day when they settled into the house together, alone.

Maybe tonight she'd let Brody take her camera in the bedroom and turn the tables a bit.

She'd never let anyone take any kind of sexy photograph of her, ever. But she was about to marry the man after all. It might be fun.

Fun, she mused, was getting easier for her.

Lost in thought, she didn't notice at first that Brody was motioning her over to the stock car he'd been showing the guys. They weren't allowed to drive it, but it had been a charge for them seeing it up close. Brody had gotten permission for them to drive their own cars around the track a few times, though, and had videoed them and given each of them feedback and things to improve on. The kids ate up every word.

Now they were sitting back, eating sandwiches and grinning at her as she approached the group.

"What?" she asked, looking at them all suspiciously.

"Your turn," Brody said.

"What? My turn to do what?"

"Drive."

"That?" she asked incredulously, pointing at the stock car.

Brody laughed. "Sure, why not? I dare you."

Hannah set a hand on her hip, glaring at him. "I don't think so."

"It's a scaled-down model, a very standard stock car, really. I couldn't let the guys drive it because of their age, and since they don't hold their own insurance, but you do. And besides, it's my car. I can say who drives it and who doesn't."

"You're really enjoying this, aren't you?" she said, shaking her head at him.

"I am. You will, too. You've been in a car with me before, you know how great it is."

"I was a passenger. And it was somewhat terrifying."

"So I'll be the passenger this time. We'll take a few turns around until you get a feel for it, and then you can see if you want to go faster. Completely up to you."

"C'mon, Hannah, you can do it!" The young

kids behind her cheered her on, telling her not to be chicken. She rolled her eyes, but gave in.

"Fine, I can drive it around, but I'm not going fast," she said.

Brody winked at her. "I bet you do."

She started to set her camera down, and Brody put out his hand. "Let me take that. I can get a few shots of you while you drive."

She smiled, reflecting on her earlier thoughts about letting him take pictures of her. This wasn't what she'd had in mind, but she handed him the camera anyway. He'd gotten some nice shots of her with Zip the other day, and had even asked to have one he could frame. Hannah had been very touched by that.

What was she worried about? All she had to do was drive the car around the track a few times. It wasn't Daytona, but a smaller, local track, and far less intimidating. She could do this.

"Let's go, then," she said cheerfully, getting into the driver's seat and taking the helmet Brody provided.

She'd worn the five-point harness seat belt before, and started to adjust it to her size when Brody reached over.

"Let me help with that," he offered.

As he did so, she knew it was no mistake when the back of his hand grazed her breast, or touched her arm, his fingers brushing her neck.

"You may want to stop that unless you want me to wreck your car," she said drily, her heart racing at each touch.

"Good point," he said, and then ran her through some basics, because once they were driving, it would be impossible to talk. They had helmets but not wired ones. "You don't have to go fast. I was only kidding you. Just have fun, sweetheart."

She nodded and they started out, rolling onto the straightaway, where Hannah drove the car up to highway speeds, but at the curve slowed down a little, getting a feel for it.

On the next stretch, she went faster, but no more so than she would on a regular interstate, again slowing down for the curve, but not as much. Hannah didn't want to take unnecessary chances, but the car handled well, and she was feeling more comfortable.

She looked over at Brody, who gave her the thumbs-up, then pointed to his eyes and back at the track, reminding her to stay focused. Hannah started feeling more confident, picking up speed until she looked down and saw her current speed on the straightaway—105 miles an hour!

Her eyes widened. She'd gone that fast—faster— with Brody driving, but this was *her* at the wheel. *One more time.* She bit her lip in concentration as she slowed on the curve, remembering all of the instructions she'd heard Brody giving the boys.

She concentrated on the track, following her instincts as she let off the gas but didn't hit the brake. As soon as she came out of it, she put her foot down on the pedal, holding her breath and spiking the speed to 125 until they roared back to the spot where they'd started.

The guys at the side were jumping up and down, cheering, as Hannah rolled the car to a stop.

Her insides felt as if they were shaking from the adrenaline rush, which seemed to take over her entire body. She'd never imagined that she could be in control of such speed and power. Or that she would enjoy it so much.

Brody was smiling at her as though she was made of gold.

"I *knew* it. I knew you'd be awesome," he said, leaning over to kiss her, but their helmets made that somewhat difficult until she took hers off.

Then he kissed her properly, grinning widely as he pulled back and got out of the car.

Hannah was still shaking with excitement. "That was…indescribable. I can see why you love it so much. That feeling, that rush… There can't be anything in the world that compares."

He gazed at her so deeply, so seriously, and she thought he was about to say something, but then Aiden appeared in the car window along with his friends, all of them chattering at once.

As they helped Hannah slide out of the car, she had to brace herself on the door; her knees were weak when they hit the pavement. She wasn't sure if it was the drive or the kiss or that look in Brody's eyes a few minutes ago, but it had all shaken her to the core—in the best possible way.

As they drove home, she thought about all the adventures that lay ahead of her, but she wasn't sure if anything could ever compare to this time with Brody.

And that worried her very much.

THE NEXT MORNING, Brody skimmed through the pictures he'd taken of Hannah in the car the day before, sipping his coffee as he studied them. He loved the fierce concentration on her face, the focus she held as she took a curve, her jubilant expression as she brought the car to a stop. Her face shone with such surprise and joy that his heart skipped slightly. Right now, across the table from him, her attention was on the laptop screen with the same amazing focus.

This had become their de facto morning routine. After they got out of bed—sometimes sooner, sometimes later—they had breakfast, took care of the horses and then came back to sit down with more coffee while she worked on her blog and he took care of other business. Or sometimes Brody read the news, if he didn't have reason to leave the house.

It was too easy to think of this being a permanent arrangement, but it wasn't. In fact, the sooner they could find a reason to dissolve their marriage, the better it would be for both of them, especially once he returned to the track.

"What are you doing?" he asked, curious about what had her fingers flying so quickly over the keyboard.

She seemed dazed for a moment, her focus broken, and then she smiled at him.

"I put up a blog about driving yesterday, and I'm responding to the comments. So many of them. I never realized how many people fantasized about doing this. I was researching the driving experience sites, and there are a lot of places where people can go to drive supercars or race on a track, and someone suggested I visit them and do a series of reviews of the various venues. That could be a great project. I could structure my travels around visiting each location, starting a tour of race-track experience locations a month or so after the wedding, perhaps."

"That's an interesting idea. I could set you up with some people I know, if that would help."

"Thanks, but it's important for me to do this on my own, you know?"

Brody nodded. He was happy for Hannah—very much so. He almost told her that he had already helped her out, just once—the first editor who had contacted her had been a friend of his. He wanted to do whatever he could to help her push forward with her new life, her new adventures. Her new career. The one that would take her away from him, eventually.

Suddenly, that didn't sit as well as it should have. While he lounged here imagining sunny mornings in the kitchen and settling into routines, she was already making plans for her new life. It was as if they had reversed positions, and while she was picking up speed, he was slowing down. The things that had never appealed to him before—being home, being *stuck*—were now much more desirable.

Maybe it was because of the person he was stuck with.

But the moment to tell her about his contact passed, and he let it go. It didn't mean anything anyway. If she hadn't had good material, it never would have been accepted.

The phone rang, and he tensed. Probably another reporter.

But when he looked, he saw it was Jud Harris, and picked up the call.

"Jud, what can I do for you?"

"I know this is somewhat last minute, Brody, but we'd like to throw a small cocktail party tonight at seven. For you and your fiancée. We'd like to meet her; this engagement has been a great idea. The press has been running nothing but positive media about you two for several days. I hope you plan to have coverage at the wedding?"

Jud's invitation wasn't a request, it was a command, and Brody bridled. He knew this was part of the deal. He'd lived his life knowing he had to make certain public appearances and had glad-handed more than one corporate sponsor, playing the game so that he could get back to doing what he loved most, and he was always good at it.

But now…it felt wrong. Unsavory. As if it was making a mockery of his relationship with Hannah. Making it shallow.

But that was the reality of it, wasn't it? He'd started believing his own lies, he supposed.

Hannah was moving forward, making plans.

He needed to keep his eye on the ball, too.

"Sure, Jud, give me the address." Brody ignored the question about reporters at the wedding for now.

He scratched the address on the pad of paper on the counter, knowing the spot. He'd been there before for business events, and it wasn't far.

"We'll see you at seven."

Jud, appeased, hung up, and Brody stood by the counter, unsure what to do next.

"I think I'm going to call Aiden to see if he wants to work on the car. Since I'll be away more come November, I want to spend more time with him now, getting it started. Then maybe he can keep tinkering with it when I'm back to the circuit."

Hannah looked up, smiling. "Sounds wonderful.

It's great how you're bonding with him. He seems happy."

Brody nodded, feeling a pang of disappointment. What did he think, that she would beg him to stick around? That she wanted to spend time with him as much as he did with her?

This was all wrong. This wasn't him, to be so needy. He'd clearly lost perspective, and he wanted to get it back. He had to get some distance, as Hannah had wisely pointed out earlier.

Still, it would have been nice if she had been at least a little reluctant to see him leave.

"We have an event tonight, as well. That was my publicist with the sponsor. They want to meet you, so they're throwing a cocktail party at a local place. You okay with that?"

"Sure. I know it's part of the deal. I'll have to shop, I suppose. I don't have anything to wear to that kind of thing, and I want to make a good impression, of course."

Brody crossed the kitchen, tipping her chin up with his fingers as he looked down into her face.

"You could show up in a burlap bag and be perfect," he said, leaning down to capture her lips in a quick kiss.

But he knew by now that when he was kissing Hannah, quick was never possible. Incredibly, he only seemed to want more of her. He told himself it was the situation, and they were only together a short time. It would wear off eventually, for both of them.

But not right now, he thought as he leaned over her in her chair so he could deepen the kiss. Then he decided Aiden could wait for a while, pulling Hannah to the kitchen floor with him, as she gasped and laughed.

She was sprawled over him, wearing some wisp of a sundress, which he was thankful for, since that made it easy to reach all of the things he wanted.

Looking up, he took in how the sun was now shining through her hair as it fell around her face, her lips parted, eyes bright with anticipation. She was already working the zipper on his jeans, staring at him with all of that lovely intensity she always gave to whatever she was doing.

On this, they were in exactly the same place. Her desire equaled his, and that thrilled him. Hannah didn't say anything as she lowered herself over him, taking him in completely. For Brody, for that moment, everything in the world was right again.

11

LATER THAT EVENING, the world had tipped on its axis, the peaceful time she had been enjoying with Brody evaporating.

Hannah tugged at the hem of her dress as Brody held the door of the Charger open, allowing her to get out. It felt too short, or maybe her heels were too high. Was her lipstick the wrong color? She took one more peek in the rearview mirror before turning her attention to the sprawling, Southern plantation–style mansion in front of them.

A flash blinded her for a moment—another reporter grabbing a picture of her and Brody as he closed the door, his other hand poised protectively at the small of her back. Hannah didn't mind having her picture taken, but this was getting ridiculous.

She'd had no idea being in the public eye would be so…public. On top of that, her blog had almost crashed, but in a good way, and she was up most of the night posting new content as well as picking out which pictures to send to another magazine that had asked for photos from her.

She'd sent them, on a whim, a few pictures of Brody and his teenage group out by their cars, teaching the young men the ropes. The editor had loved them and wanted more to show her boss. Everything was happening at once, and Hannah could barely balance on these heels, let alone balance everything that was happening around her.

Brody, however, didn't seem ruffled at all, not even breaking a sweat, though it was a very warm evening. At the moment, his eyes seemed to be glued to her legs as she wobbled slightly and put a hand on his shoulder to get her balance. Why had she let Brandi talk her into these shoes? Hannah never wore more than a one-inch, solid heel, but she supposed the way Brody kept looking at her made every precarious step worth it.

"I may need you to stick close so I don't end up teetering over and making a fool of myself," she joked, not quite hiding her nerves as they walked up to the grand entrance.

Brody slipped an arm around her waist, pulling her in closer. That did help, as always.

"You could never do that. You look amazing... Those shoes and that skirt," he whispered in her ear, "are making me crazy. I don't know if I'll last the whole evening until we can get back home and I can peel that off you."

He nipped her earlobe, making her gasp lightly as he pressed the doorbell, the immediate arousal distracting her from her nerves.

The door opened, and given the lush setting, she almost expected to see women in hoop skirts from *Gone with the Wind* on the other side, but instead a man in his fifties, she estimated, greeted them with a smile. He was handsome, but in a slick, superficial kind of way, Hannah thought. His hands were too smooth when he shook hers.

"Brody, so good to see you. This must be Hannah," he said, smiling at her while his eyes took her in from head to toe, though not in a lascivious way.

More as if he was assessing her market value.

"Jud, good to see you, too," Brody said, his hand tightening slightly on Hannah's waist.

"Sorry about the short notice," Jud said as he stepped back, motioning for them to come in, "but we couldn't let your announcement go without some kind of celebration. This certainly happened out of the blue, but I can see why you'd want to snap up Hannah before she got away."

"It was a spontaneous thing," Brody agreed coolly.

Jud closed the door and faced them. "Most of the higher-ups in the company and other guests are in the garden room, and we expect a few more guests shortly. The media have been invited as well, as you can see. They are allowed to circulate freely—the more exposure the better for this. Come on in and say hello."

Jud led the way, and they followed. Hannah caught her breath as they moved into the next room. The garden room was a gorgeous solarium that allowed the dappled sunlight that made its way through the trees and gardens outside the room to reach all of the tropical plants that filled the inside, as well.

"Oh, this is lovely," Hannah couldn't help but comment, and Jud faced her, smiling.

"Thank you. It's one of our company's favorite

properties. The place was quite a mess when we picked it up. In fact, it was set for demolition. We bought it and renovated it as a historic landmark for the area and use as it an executive vacation home, as well as for special events, like this one."

"That's very generous of you. Many corporations wouldn't care about something like that."

Jud smiled, and eyed Brody. "I guess you could say we're always interested in saving things we think are worth the effort."

Brody stiffened slightly, and Hannah grabbed his hand, squeezing it as they walked to a long white table at the front of the room. Hannah felt all eyes turn in their direction. She supposed she was going to have to get used to that, at least for a while.

"I don't know how you've done it," she said to Brody in a low tone.

"What's that?"

"Lived in the public eye for so long. It's disconcerting. At the diner, here…everywhere."

"You get used to it," he said. "The next few days will be busy, but after that, it will quiet down again."

"Until you return to the track, of course," Jud said quietly, obviously overhearing their conversation. "I assume you know about that?" he asked Hannah in the same hushed tone.

She nodded. Brody had already told Jud this, but apparently he felt the need to confirm. Jud hadn't been happy about it, apparently, but Brody hadn't given him a choice. That was the reason for this get-together, she figured. Not to celebrate, but to size her up and make sure she knew the score.

"Of course, you understand no one else can know anything about this," he said to her unnecessarily.

"Of course," Hannah echoed coolly.

Jud didn't know their marriage was not a real one, though she didn't think he'd care, either. The guy was not made of sincerity. If this worked for Brody's image, that was all that mattered.

Someone handed her a glass of champagne, and she smiled a thank-you, though drinking was probably not a wise option, especially since she hadn't had dinner yet.

As she took the glass, Jud's eyes went to her hand. "No ring yet?"

It was all Hannah could do not to roll her eyes. The topic of the missing engagement ring had come up constantly. There were actual debates online about it on the racing fan boards.

"I really didn't want one," she said. "We'll have gold bands, and that's enough for me."

"A ring would play better in the press, and in the pictures," Jud said, mostly to Brody.

"I'm not marrying the press," Brody said, smiling at Jud, but there was a warning in his eyes.

"Well, then, I suppose we should spin it as Hannah being an independent, modern woman who isn't attached to material things, but some of your fans might not be impressed by that," he said.

"I don't really give a damn," Brody said, almost making Hannah laugh out loud, given her earlier thoughts about the Margaret Mitchell setting.

She bit back the laugh, coughing instead, and both men turned to her.

"Excuse me, I guess this went down the wrong

way," she said, smiling sweetly as she took a small sip from her glass. The double entendre was clear, and she saw the publicist's lips tighten in disapproval while Brody's grin stretched wide.

"Let's make some introductions, and then we can have a toast, as I think most of the press are here," Jud said. Hannah was pretty sure that he wanted this over with as much as she did. Then he said, "Oh, and we also need to talk about your blog, Hannah. And how we can leverage that to help get positive exposure for Brody. You're getting a great response, but we have to be careful about what we post there. Certain pictures might not convey the right…direction. It needs a better title for one thing, and a press page."

Hannah was stunned silent, as was Brody.

"Hannah's blog is not part of my PR campaign, Jud. It's off-limits. She does what she wants there," Brody said plainly.

"She's going to be your wife. Everything she does, especially if it includes publishing pictures of you with kids involved in illegal racing or getting involved in fights, reflects on you," Jud responded, and then cut the conversation short as someone approached and he pasted on his smile, introducing them to some corporate clone.

They made the rounds of the room and smiled for the cameras, which got exhausting pretty quickly. But Hannah did her best—this was the deal, helping Brody with his public image while seeking out new adventures for herself.

Not that this was all that adventurous. It was actually deadly boring.

She aimed to fix that, and when they had a break,

she took Brody's hand, leading him away down a hall when no one was looking. In the middle of all of this fakery, she needed something honest. She needed Brody.

"Where are we going?"

She smiled at him. "I thought it might be nice to go outside for a breath of fresh air."

He heard her loud and clear, and smiled back. "Yeah, these guys do suck the air out of a room, don't they? I didn't think Jud would be coming on this strong," he said apologetically. "He's being a real jerk tonight. Don't take anything he says about your blog seriously."

Not that Hannah intended to let anyone dictate what her work would be—she'd had more than enough of that for years—but she appreciated Brody's support and intended to show him how much. They emerged into the elaborate gardens and walked more slowly, losing themselves amid the winding paths. It was humid, but there was a pleasant, evening breeze. Tree frogs were chirping, and they discovered a screened gazebo at the end of one path, far away from the house and surrounded by dense vegetation. Completely out of view.

Exactly what she wanted.

"Hannah, are you okay?" he asked in reply to her silence. "I know Jud's comments about your blog were out of line. I can't believe he actually thought—"

She kissed him then, stopping his words. Hannah didn't want to talk about Jud or anyone else. She wanted to be with Brody and to remind herself, and him, why they were in the middle of this situation anyway.

It didn't take more than a second for Brody to respond in kind, walking her back against a post, where he took over the kiss, which Hannah didn't mind at all.

"You taste like champagne," he whispered. "So this is why you wanted to get away?"

"I wanted something…real," she said, kissing him again and reaching down to take his hand, sliding it up under the hem of her dress.

Hannah, in another daring moment—they were becoming more frequent for her, definitely—had worn the dress with nothing underneath.

She was going to tell Brody before they went in the house, but had forgotten, and now she helped him discover her secret for himself.

"Oh, darlin'… Oh, yeah," he growled against her mouth at the discovery, his hand slipping around to cup the curve of her bare backside, pulling her against his hardness. "That's real, for sure."

Hannah gave herself over, wrapping her arms around his neck, wanting to forget everything but how Brody felt and how he made her feel.

His fingers stroked between her legs, drawing whimpers from her, and he kissed her to help silence them, swallowing her moans as she came apart in his arms. While she tried to catch her breath, he did it again, and Hannah could only hold on tight.

But as her mind cleared, she found the zipper on his slacks, opened it and slid her fingers inside.

"You're so hard," she sighed. "I love touching you."

"The feeling's mutual, sweetheart," he managed, his breathing reflecting how turned on he was.

Hannah loved how he surged against her, pushing

into her hand, all hot, tense and full of need. Need that she planned on sating, as he had hers.

Dropping down, she braced her back against the post for balance and took him in her mouth before he could argue. Once she did, he couldn't say anything but her name.

Hannah loved undoing him like this; it made her feel powerful, purely female. She kissed and touched him with tenderness as a desperate need welled inside of her to please him, to give him whatever she could.

"Hannah, sweetheart, you need to… I'm going to…"

She answered by taking him deeper, knowing what he was trying to say and only wanting him to let go completely for her the way she had for him. He had no choice—a second later he came, shuddering in her arms.

Hannah didn't want this to end; she wanted as much of him as she could have, but when he tipped her face up, she smiled against his shoulder.

"You are the most incredible woman in the world," he said, sounding very emotional.

"I know," she said cheekily, trying to lighten the mood, enjoying how his chest rumbled with laughter in response.

"I have to say, while the fake retirement is a pain, and I can't wait until it's over and I'm back on the track, being with you, Hannah… Marrying you… It doesn't feel fake at all. You said you wanted something real, but everything with you is real. I know we agreed our arrangement would be temporary until I resumed racing, but—"

Hannah's heart was heavy as she wondered what

he was about to say when a group of people rounded the corner, chatting and laughing, making Brody turn. He frowned, and with a sigh, didn't finish what he was going to tell her.

"Time to act the happily engaged couple for a while longer, and then get the heck out of here?"

"Sure, let's go," she said brightly, but her happiness dimmed at his words, chilling some of the warmth they'd shared. But as they reentered the party, she put on a smile, like he did, and played her part.

THE NEXT MORNING, Brody walked down to the stables to get the horses out, since he hadn't slept a wink. Hannah had eventually passed out, and he'd let her sleep. She'd been quiet on the drive home from the party, though when he asked her if she was okay, she'd reassured him she was.

Brody's instincts were telling him something else was bothering her, but if she didn't want to talk about it, he was okay with that, too.

The horses were calm in the cool, early morning, happy to be out in the pasture. Even Zip went along with him easily, as if knowing Brody had enough on his mind.

In the corral, Brody paused to stand with the horse that had thrown him, and whispered a thank-you to the big beast. His back injury, now more or less healed, was the reason Hannah had shown up here in the first place. Brody was having an increasingly difficult time thinking about life without her. He patted Zip on the shoulder.

"I guess we'll both have to get used to being without her at some point," he said to the horse, who had definitely taken a liking to Hannah.

Zip did something amazing then, taking a few steps closer to Brody as he moved away, as if not wanting him to go. Brody gave him another pat, and Zip returned the gesture with the same affectionate nudge the horse had offered Hannah on numerous occasions.

Brody paused, wondering if Zip wasn't issuing an invitation. Hannah had read him correctly. For whatever reason, Zip didn't like being saddled. She'd ridden him bareback several times now, and Zip had behaved like a gentleman.

While he knew he was taking a risk, Brody gave in to curiosity and hauled himself up on Zip's back, giving him a soft kick with his heel. The horse took off in a gentle trot. Brody laughed, patting Zip's neck.

"Good man, Zip."

They rode for a half hour without incident. Then Brody slipped down from Zip, patting him on the backside. The horse took off into the field, when the sound of a powerful engine rumbled down from the driveway.

Who could that be? It didn't sound like Aiden's car—in fact, it sounded like the smooth growl of a Ferrari Italia, if he wasn't mistaken, and Brody rarely was when it came to cars.

Sure enough, as Brody climbed back up the hill, he saw the gleaming red Italian sports car parked by his Charger and let out a resounding whoop as he saw who was standing next to it.

Reece Winston and his wife, Abby, both waved

and smiled as Brody quickened his step, closing the distance.

"Hey, I thought you were in France!"

Reece returned the quick hug Brody offered, and then Abby, as Brody stood back, taking in the car.

"Yours?"

"Of course."

"Beauty. Let's get her out on the track today."

"Guys, *seriously*?" Abby intervened, pulling them back to the moment.

Brody laughed. "I'm glad you're here, but we thought you wouldn't be able to make the wedding."

Reece was about to speak, but Abby interjected again. "You are two of our best friends. Do you really think we'd miss your I dos?"

"Well, I'm very glad you could make it," Brody said, rubbing a hand over his face.

"When Abby told me the news, I wasn't sure I could get back in time, but I found someone at the last minute to take over for me on the renovation from the damage, and we got down here as soon as we could. I couldn't miss this. Where's Hannah?"

Brody looked back toward the house. "She was sleeping. I was taking care of the horses, but usually she's up by now. We had an event last night that really took it out of her, though."

"You okay, Brody? You look...tense."

"Probably wedding nerves," Abby said, taking her husband by the arm. "This is a gorgeous place. Hannah said so, but I can see why you wanted to retire here."

Brody nodded, and then he was saved from saying anything more about his giving up racing when the front door opened. Hannah appeared and came running down from the porch. She threw herself into a hug that Abby had waiting.

"I can't believe you're here! This is such a great surprise!"

Abby stood back and took in Hannah with a big smile. "I wouldn't miss this for the world, but you two still have to come up to the vineyard for a celebration this summer."

Brody and Hannah shared a look, and Brody noticed Hannah didn't say anything to that, either, and instead invited Reece and Abby in for breakfast.

As they settled into the kitchen, Hannah poured coffee and Brody pulled some bowls out of a cupboard, grabbing ingredients for pancakes.

"Wow, I don't think I've ever seen you so domestic," Reece commented. "Female hearts are breaking all over the world today." Brody sent a wet sponge from the counter sailing by his head.

"Any self-respecting man should be able to make pancakes," Brody declared. "I can fry a mean egg, too, but not as good as Hannah's."

Hannah sent him a happy smile and kissed his cheek as she passed by him to get two more coffees, making Brody forget what he was measuring. She always did that to him. He watched her cute little backside as she walked over to the coffeepot until Abby cleared her throat, and Brody realized he'd been caught peeking.

"Hey, buddy, eyes on the pancakes," Abby said with mock severity.

"They were," Brody replied without missing a beat,

sending all of them except for Hannah into spontaneous laughter.

"What's so funny?"

"Nothing, babe, just being harassed by the peanut gallery."

"The pancake gallery, you mean," Reece added.

The fun continued as they ate breakfast, and Brody relaxed into it, enjoying the company. It was always nice to have good friends around.

"Okay, these pancakes are the best ever," Abby said, reaching for another from the platter at the center of the table.

"Hey," Reece responded. "I thought my pancakes were your favorite?"

"A girl can never have too many pancakes," Hannah intervened, and then more laughter broke out, leaving her mystified again.

"I'll explain later," Brody promised, leaning in to catch some syrup from the corner of her lip.

"You two are almost disgustingly sweet together," Reece said with a pained sigh.

"Oh, really? You don't remember how moony you both were back when you met?" Brody challenged, grinning. "I thought I'd get a cavity."

It had only been a year or so since he and Hannah had sat at breakfast in Daytona with Reece and Abby, watching them navigate the ups and downs of their budding romance. They'd faced some challenges back then, but their love for each other had been stronger than any of it. Now they looked so perfectly happy together that Brody knew Reece had made the right choice, though they'd had a tough start, for sure.

"So we know you two didn't want to make any

fuss, but Reece and I would at least like to take you to dinner tonight, somewhere nice, to celebrate. We made reservations at a local place, and we won't take no for an answer."

"That's sweet of your both, thank you," Hannah said, reaching over to squeeze Abby's hand, and that was when Abby noticed Hannah's hand, too.

"No ring?"

"Why is everyone so focused on the ring?" Hannah asked incredulously.

"I bought her a camera instead," Brody said, deadpan.

"What?" Abby and Reece responded in kind.

Hannah sighed. "I really don't want an engagement ring—and believe me, the camera he bought me is as expensive as any diamond. We'll wear gold bands, and that's enough for me. I don't want people thinking I'm marrying him for his money."

"No one will think *that's* why you're marrying me, honey," Brody said with a lascivious grin, making Hannah slap him in the arm, turning bright red.

As they visited some more and cleaned up, Brody insisted that their friends stay with them, but Reece declined.

"We already grabbed a room at an inn close by, and you guys are newlyweds, or will be shortly. You should be here by yourselves," he pointed out, making Hannah blush again.

Brody was secretly relieved. It would be easier this way. As much as he loved Reece and Abby, having them stay at the house meant he and Hannah would have to be careful about everything they said, and they'd also have to make sure they kept up the pretense of their situation.

Though curiously, none of this seemed like pretense. At least not the past few hours with their friends. In some ways, he thought, maybe that was worse.

"Hey, you okay?" Hannah asked quietly as they put some dishes away.

"Great, yeah, why?"

"Just… You looked kind of sad, I guess."

Brody shook his head. "Nope, I'm fine, honestly," he replied, kissing her lightly before turning back to their guests.

But he knew he was lying again—to Hannah, in part—and to himself. However, that was a lot easier than considering the truth.

It was getting too easy to believe all of this was real, and he had to guard against that. They both did, because in the end, they wouldn't be like Reece and Abby, and that was okay. He and Hannah had different goals.

Suddenly, though, those goals seemed less and less appealing.

12

"WHAT THE…?" HANNAH SAID on an exhale as she saw the parking lot crammed with every kind of sport and exotic car she could imagine.

"I guess it was hard to hide the surprise for too long," Abby said with a barely smothered grin.

Hannah gaped. "You mean…all of this is for *us*? I thought we were just having dinner."

Hannah had suspected that Abby and Reece might have invited Brody's family as well, but she'd never expected anything like what was facing her now.

"It took a bit of doing to contact everyone, but it's really only our families and a lot of Brody's friends from racing… It's only about sixty people or so."

"Oh, only sixty?" Hannah said weakly.

"C'mon, it'll be fun. There's a surprise for you," Abby said, dragging Hannah forward.

Once they were inside, Hannah knew what it was the moment she heard her name across the room.

"Hannah and Brody, there you are!"

Her mom walked quickly in their direction, and Hannah covered her mouth with her hands, so shocked that she couldn't say anything for a second. She was always happy to see her mom, but hadn't expected her until tomorrow.

"Mom, how long have you been down here?"

"Only since last weekend. Abby needed feet on the ground to check out venues and get things set up, so Lynn and I worked together."

"Lynn? Brody's mom? You've met already? Wait… you mean, you guys have been planning this since—"

"Since you told us, yes! Reece did have some delays getting back, but Abby and I were on the phone immediately, planning. Do you think we'd just show up at the last minute? And now I need to meet my future son-in-law," she said, turning to Brody.

"Mrs. Morgan, so nice to meet you at last," he said, accepting and returning the hug Hannah's mom offered.

"Mrs. Morgan? *Please*, Brody, we're about to be family. Call me Trish."

He nodded, smiling warmly at her mother. "Trish it is."

Hannah watched as her mom put her arm through Brody's and walked away with him, winking at Hannah. As they parted, she did, however, overhear her mom say, "So now let's talk about why Hannah isn't wearing a ring."

"Point me to the bar?" Hannah asked Abby with a tense smile.

HER FRIEND PULLED her into the fray. "Over here, c'mon."

Hannah was aware of Abby watching her closely as she ordered her beer from the open bar. Abby ordered only a soda.

"You don't want a drink?"

"Nah, maybe later. You know I never drink at a party I've organized. Have to make sure everything goes perfectly," Abby said with a too-bright smile.

Hannah suspected her friend was hiding yet another surprise. Shrugging, she took a deep swig of her lager, scanning the room to see where her mom had hidden Brody.

"Hannah, what's going on?"

"What do you mean?"

"You're so anxious I can almost feel it. Even allowing for bridal nerves, you seem…off. Is everything okay?"

Hannah took a breath and realized she *was* tense, and she was being less than appreciative of a friend who had gone above and beyond to throw this party. The celebration was perfect, but it also put Hannah in exactly the position she'd been trying to avoid.

"I'm sorry, Abby. I guess this has all been fast. I'm barely used to the idea of getting married, and we wanted to keep things small, no fuss. But there was a party last night, which was exhausting, and now this—which is totally wonderful but also… overwhelming."

"I understand. But try to enjoy it—you only get to do this once, if you do it right," Abby said with a grin. "And from the way you two look at each other, I think it's very right. I couldn't be happier for you, Hannah. Who knew when you headed out on the road, you would end up in a wedding with Brody?"

Hannah put down her drink and hugged her friend, wishing so much she could tell her everything. Abby was the best, and it felt wrong not to let her know, but that was what Brody had meant when they'd gotten into this whole thing. How heavy the lies could become. She couldn't tell Abby about the marriage arrangement without spilling the beans about Brody's retirement, so that was that.

"Hey, don't hog the bride," a male voice accused.

Hannah saw Reece, looking amazing in a Tom Ford suit, coming in to hug her. Behind him was a group of professional racing personalities that was enough to make any girl's head spin, lined up to congratulate her and Brody.

Everyone cycled through, wishing them the best, hugging and shaking hands and telling a lot of jokes, of course. All of the warmth and cheer should have been buoying, but instead, Hannah was struggling to maintain her smile each time, eventually excusing herself to get some air.

Brody followed her out to a veranda at the back that was a lot less crowded, and Hannah took several deep breaths.

"You okay, babe?"

She nodded and then shook her head, covering her face with both hands.

"I can't believe they did this, and it must have cost Reece and Abby a fortune, and everyone is so wonderful and sweet, and it makes me feel like the worst person ever."

Brody's frown was deep when she lowered her hands, and he took them in his.

"I know what you mean," he said, his eyes dark with concern, and something else. "I hate seeing you unhappy, and I hate this whole situation. That's why I've made a decision. It's too late for it to matter in terms of this party, but…I'm calling Jud in the morning and telling him I'm out. I quit. I'm not doing this anymore. I'll take my lumps, and I'll get back into racing on my own somehow. It's what I should have done in the first place. I don't need them."

Hannah's jaw dropped.

"What? No! You can't do that… The pressure is getting to you, Brody, which is completely understandable, but it's just a few more months, and then you'll be back driving, and that's all you've ever wanted to do."

"I'm not so sure about that anymore, Hannah. I'm not sure about anything right now, except that you're under all this stress, and everyone here is celebrating a lie, and it's all to support this…this ruse that the sponsor cooked up. I was wrong to ever agree to go along with it in the first place."

"Brody, listen, don't do anything rash until we can talk more—"

"Hey, lovebirds, you're missing your own party," Reece said cheerfully, and then lost his smile as he took in both of their expressions. "What's wrong?"

Hannah smiled brightly and took Brody's hand.

"Nothing is wrong, promise. This is such a lovely thing to do, Reece. We can't thank you enough. You and Abby are such good friends."

She squeezed Brody's hand, willing him to go along with her. Hannah understood his feelings, but she couldn't let him throw everything away because she was having a momentary meltdown. His career meant everything to him, and he was just having a bad moment.

He'd change his mind after he calmed down, and

agree that she was right. Until then, she had to make
sure that she kept it together, too, for his sake, as well
as for her own. He was so upset because of her, and
she appreciated that.

"It's a party," she said cheerfully. "Let's go have
some fun!"

Reece whooped. "Now, that's what I'm talking
about. And if Brody can't dance with his bad back,
Hannah, I know about thirty guys willing to take his
place for the evening."

Brody frowned and Hannah laughed.

"No one could ever take his place, Reece," she said,
and amid all the lies they were telling, those words
came from the heart.

BY MORNING, BRODY was even more certain about what
he had to do to make things right. He was going to
call Jud after breakfast and take his knocks, getting
this over with. He'd be without a sponsor, and without
a car or team, until he could figure out the finances.
Whoever wanted to stay with him, and whoever
wanted to leave, he would hold no grudges against
anyone.

Including Hannah. He could stop all of this before
she made a huge mistake, trying to help him, as well.

His hands actually turned a bit cold at the thought.
What next? He wasn't sure. But this had gone far
enough. He'd let it all happen, and only he could stop
it.

Brody paused and looked over the farm—his home,
his family's home—and thought about how he'd been
living in limbo, only half of himself really here. The
rest of him was living in the future, waiting for some

magical point when he'd have his career back. But if lying to people he loved was the price of getting it back, it was too high. It was time to move on.

To…something.

Whatever it was, he needed to be in it 100 percent, making his own decisions, not letting others dictate how he acted, who he slept with, what he chose to do with his life.

Who he was.

He needed to let Hannah off the hook, let her follow her own star. But maybe that didn't mean letting her go altogether, he thought hopefully. They didn't need to get married, right?

Dropping the sponsor would mean they didn't have to get married, but he didn't want her out of his life. He just had to make sure everyone knew it was his fault. Not Hannah's.

He had been, for all of the craziness, looking forward to marrying Hannah. But now there'd be no reason for her to do that, would there? The thought landed hard, and somewhat painfully, in his chest.

"Brody?"

Hannah emerged on the porch, holding Brody's phone in her hand, looking sleepy. His phone must have awakened her, and he reached for it.

"Sorry, hon, I should have brought it out with me."

"It's Jud Harris. He sounds…angry."

Brody frowned as he took the phone from her hand.

"Jud, good timing. I was going to call you after breakfast."

"So you know already?"

"Know what?"

"About the story in the rag sheet? You and your

fiancée." Jud said the word with a sleazy emphasis that made Brody's spine straighten.

"What are you talking about?"

"You both made the cover of the *National Intruder*, as well as going viral on the internet. How could you be so stupid? Getting in some woman's skirt out in the gazebo? Doing it on company property? During an event? Are you nuts? The bosses are furious."

Brody tried to interrupt, to find out what exactly Jud was saying, but he kept rolling.

"Then talking about the retirement contract *in public*? And what is this about a temporary marriage? Who *is* Hannah anyway? Some kind of call girl? Someone you paid to marry you?"

The world spun and Brody raced to catch up. "You watch yourself, Jud—"

"Forget it, Brody. Do you know the mess you've created? There's not much I can do. I'll be lucky if I don't lose my job over this. Our reply to this is going to be that this was all you, bud. That this publicity stunt was your idea, and we just hoped you could clean up your act. Your sponsorship is gone, and as far as we're concerned, we knew nothing about any of it."

The line went dead, and Brody had to pause for several seconds, shell-shocked and unsure what he was going to do when he turned back to Hannah.

Brody didn't know exactly what had happened, but he was able to glean enough from the conversation to guess.

Someone from the media must have followed them at the cocktail party, taken pictures, listening in when he and Hannah had had their tryst.

He wanted to punch something—namely, he

wanted to punch Jud square in the face, which was probably what he should have done at the start of this mess.

But Jud wasn't responsible for all of it, was he? Brody had gone along, and then he'd dragged Hannah down with him. There was no more comeback, no more sponsorship. Ironic that after all of this, as soon as he had decided to bow out, his retirement had now become real and his life was falling apart.

He'd take his lumps and shoulder the blame, but what he cared about most was Hannah and how he could protect her from the storm that was coming.

Even worse, he knew, was that he probably couldn't.

They'd been reckless, no doubt. He'd been photographed in compromising positions before, many times—the sex-club fiasco came to mind—but Hannah hadn't. Brody had no idea what he could do. The tiger was already out of its cage, by the sound of it.

"Brody, what's wrong?"

He realized she'd been asking him that for several minutes, but his mind was still trying to get a grip on it all. Though he knew from her expression, as she watched him, that she could feel what was coming, and that it wasn't good.

13

HANNAH WAS STILL in her robe when she froze in front of an email from the editor who had been interested in her series of articles on street racing. She had written to tell Hannah that in light of recent events, they had to decline to publish her work. They were very sorry.

Sure, they were.

In other words, she'd lost all credibility after the fiasco that had hit a major gossip magazine website, exposing the truth about Brody's fake retirement and their temporary marriage arrangement. After that, everything toppled like dominoes. Brody's sponsor had dropped him flat, people were calling about the wedding and her blog traffic had gone wild, but for all the wrong reasons.

She'd barely gotten started on her new adventure, and she was already finished.

Hannah tried to tell herself it could be worse. The photo of her sliding Brody's hand up under her skirt in the gazebo could have been a lot more damning, considering what had happened right after that. It made her want to curl up in a ball of humiliation to think that someone had watched them.

They'd had to take the phone off the hook, and Hannah had shut down the comments function on her blog after receiving many X-rated offers from male readers.

Brody had been so angry, so upset, after seeing the picture that he'd taken off in the Charger, and Reece had gone after him, unsure if Brody was on his way to punch that reporter's lights out.

"Are you okay?" Abby asked, handing her a cup of coffee and getting one for herself.

"I think so. No, maybe not. I'm not sure," Hannah said, feeling as though the world was spinning far too fast. "I don't know what to think."

"Well, you wanted excitement, and it looks as though you got it," Abby said lightly, patting her shoulder comfortingly.

"I never imagined this. I'm so sorry… I don't even know why you're still talking to me. I should have told you, except I couldn't, not without telling you why, and that was Brody's secret. But it was so hard, hiding the truth, and then when you guys went to all that effort, all that expense last night… I feel like such a jerk."

"Hey, stop that. You're not a jerk, and neither is Brody. The party was fun, and we were glad to do it, no matter what. Though this is an awful situation. When you decide to throw caution to the wind, you really go for it, don't you?"

"Yeah, and look how well that worked out."

"Things *will* work out, Hannah. It sounds as if he was really pushed into this fake retirement fiasco. Clearly that was the sponsor's idea, even if they deny it."

"He loves racing so much. This must be killing him."

Abby reached over, covering Hannah's hand with her own.

"He'll handle it. You will, too. You and Brody still have each other, and that's the most important part. You can figure out the rest as you go."

Hannah looked at her friend incredulously. "You did get the part where this marriage was a temporary arrangement, right? None of this was ever real."

"I don't believe that. You've acted out of character, that's true, but the risks you took, they were because you love him. And it's clear that he's head over heels about you. And it's not a risk if there aren't any stakes, right?"

"Thank you. That's very comforting," Hannah said grumpily. "The thing is that the fake marriage idea, that really was *my* fault. If I hadn't blurted out to that reporter that I was his fiancée in the first place, none of this would have happened at all."

"Why *did* you do that?"

"It was…an impulse. She was there, with her overly sprayed blond hair and fancy suit, sticking that microphone in his face, and you know, I saw the kinds of women who were coming around, and they all just… They were—"

"You were jealous? You wanted to stake your claim?"

Hannah's jaw dropped. "No! It wasn't like that at all. Or maybe it was, to a degree. I don't know what we were thinking."

Abby smiled serenely, which was really starting to tick Hannah off.

"Love is like that. Turns you completely upside down. Makes you do some really stupid things. And these schemes you guys were involved in, they were kind of dumb, but you were trying to help each other. Because you really wanted to be together, underneath it all. The rest was all…complication."

"You're reading too much into it."

"Really? I thought Brody might kill someone when he saw that photo. If he didn't love you, he wouldn't have gotten that angry, right? He wasn't even that angry about the sponsor, or the flack *he* was getting. But when he saw what had been done to you… Whoa. It was pretty hot, actually," Abby said with a grin.

Hope stuttered in Hannah's heart, but she couldn't have any faith in it. Abby was only trying to comfort her.

"I'm not saying we don't care about each other—we do. But we're not in love."

"Then you really are lying to yourself," Abby responded bluntly.

"Well, it doesn't matter, does it?" Hannah said, sinking to a new low in her emotional well.

"Oh, I'd say it's the only thing that matters."

"Not when it's one-sided."

"You really believe that?"

Hannah nodded miserably. She knew Brody cared for her, but it was, effectively, her fault that his career had been lost. He might not see that yet, but it was only a matter of time.

She'd started this marriage rumor, and she was the one who had taken him out to the gazebo on that brilliant, daring exploit. Literally none of this would have happened if not for her, and he was bound to connect those dots as soon as he calmed down.

Even if they stayed together, when the racing season started and he wasn't a part of it, he would only resent her for everything.

Hannah jumped when the beep signaling a text message on her phone sounded. She thought it might be Brody, but she quailed, seeing who it was from.

"Oh, no. It's my mom. She wants me to call her right now. What do you think are the chances she knows?"

Abby sighed. "Well, you did give her that tablet for her birthday…"

"Great."

"Listen, call her back and then we're getting dressed and going out for some therapeutic shopping and lunch. And we should get pedicures."

Hannah once again thought her friend had lost her mind.

"Abby, no. I can't go out in public right now. It's like walking around with a red letter on my forehead."

Abby looked her straight in the eye as she stood. "You can, and we will. You have nothing to be ashamed of, Hannah, so stop acting like you do. I won't have my baby's godmother showing such an appalling lack of chutzpah."

Hannah opened her mouth to argue again when her brain shut her up again, catching up with what Abby had said.

"Wait, what? *Baby*?"

Abby grinned so hard Hannah forgot everything

else going on in that moment and jumped from her chair so fast she knocked it back on the floor.

"I can't believe it! You're pregnant?"

"I am. We wanted to be able to tell you in person, so we could all celebrate together."

"That's so amazing… I can't believe it. I mean, I can, but…wow. You're going to be a *mom*. And I'm going to be a godmother. Can he or she call me auntie, though? I mean, I know I'm not family, technically, but—"

"Absolutely," Abby confirmed. "You *are* family, Hannah. You've always been like a sister to me. You know that. No matter what, we'll always stick by each other, and that's why we're going out to celebrate today, okay? Don't let the trolls get you down."

"Okay, I guess." Hannah gave in. Maybe Abby was right. Not everyone cared about gossip anyway. She would have to show her face in public sometime.

"Great. I'm going to run back to the room and get some things, and we can meet back here in, say, an hour?"

Hannah nodded.

She did as Abby said, calling her mom, who didn't know anything about what had been going on, thankfully. Hannah really wanted her mother to hear it from her first. And hopefully her mother would never see that photo. She was so understanding as Hannah told her everything that Hannah ended up crying buckets while still on the phone.

"Mom, I'm sorry this cost you money to come down, and the party, and now you don't need to, and that I lied, and that—"

"Hannah, stop. I'm glad to be here, and I want to

be here for you and for Brody. Who knows what could happen by Saturday?"

Why did everyone around her seem to think this wedding was still on? Didn't they get that this was *over*?

But she wasn't going to argue with her mother on the phone, and Hannah couldn't deny that she was glad to have her mom around. That definitely made things easier to handle. If the people they loved weren't angry with them, then that was all that really mattered, right?

"Okay, Mom. Thanks. I'll see you later today, I hope, but I can't make any promises about Brody. Things are really a mess."

"Don't worry about me. You let me know what you need. It's all going to be fine, honey, don't worry."

Hannah shook her head in disbelief, hanging up the call. She had to get ready to meet Abby when she returned, though she was loath to leave the house. But things were out of her hands now, so she went and got dressed, unable to stop thinking about Brody, where he was and how he was doing. In spite of it all, and all the support from her friends and family, she craved his warmth and strength more than ever, but she wasn't sure if that would be hers again.

Her computer chimed with another email, this time from the editor who had taken her first photos, the ones from the street race. He was backing out, saying they wouldn't be running the photos, but they would still pay her a "kill fee." He'd been happy to do Brody the favor of looking at her work, but she probably should send her photos elsewhere in the future.

He'd done Brody a favor?

Hannah's mind reeled at the words.

They'd only taken her work in the first place because Brody had known the junior editor and had asked him to check out her blog.

Hannah had been so foolish.

None of this had been hers. Not really. Brody had set it up. No editor had looked at her blog and been dazzled by her photographic genius, she thought harshly. And Brody had never told her.

She felt like such a dupe, being so excited over her "success."

Hannah thought she might be sick. Certainly he meant it to be helpful, or was it more that Brody thought she'd never succeed on her own?

When she thought about it, nothing she'd done on her own had gotten her any attention. She hadn't seen it until this painfully clear moment. Why would a national magazine offer to publish her work out of the blue? Hannah had been kidding herself all along. About everything, it seemed.

Humiliated in more ways than she could keep track of, she knew she was letting Abby down, but she had to get away from all of this and think. Hannah couldn't face her friend, strangers out in public or pretend that her heart wasn't breaking into about a thousand little pieces, all of her dreams shattered.

As she was leaving, she stuck a quick note on the door, apologizing, and then got into her car and drove off. She had no idea where she was going, but as the distance increased between her and the ranch, and her friends—and Brody—so did the tears, until she couldn't drive safely anymore.

When she pulled over, she found herself parked at

the spot where she and Brody had made love in the back of her car.

She cursed as the tears became impossible to stop. She couldn't go anywhere now without that memory riding along beside her. All of what she could have had.

Letting go, Hannah gave up the fight and cried for a very long time.

BRODY LOST TRACK of how long he'd driven for, the laps falling behind him as he looped the track over and over, desperate to find some clarity. Driving until he could think straight had always been his method of working through a problem. Focusing on the speed, controlling the car and not running into a wall pushed the garbage crowding his mind to the back, allowing only what was important to the surface. Today, that process yielded only one result.

Hannah.

When he'd seen that photo from the gazebo—or more specifically, Hannah's face when she'd seen it— he'd been so angry he couldn't even think straight.

It was his fault. Having dragged her into his mess, this PR stunt, getting married— What had he been thinking? Clearly, only of himself.

He'd encouraged her to take chances, to jump in and ask questions later, to be impulsive. She probably blamed him for all of this, and she'd be right to do so.

He still had to see her. If nothing else, to apologize. He'd been so furious in that moment, he'd had to leave when he should have stayed with her. What else was new? Brody Palmer had blown it again.

Pulling the car to a stop by the finish line—he was

almost out of gas anyway—he saw Reece lying back in the seat of the Ferrari, looking as if he was napping. Reece had taken the new car on a few good laps, but then he'd become bored and let Brody run himself out.

"You finished?" Reece asked.

Brody nodded.

"Figure anything out?"

"Yeah, I think so."

Brody opened the passenger-side door, and Reece put his hand out. "Nope. Not until you hit the shower."

"Are you kidding me?"

"This is leather. Expensive leather."

"My life is chaos, and that's what you're worrying about?"

Reece cocked an eyebrow at him, as if that was a stupid question.

"I'll pay to clean the seats, Reece, but I need to get to Hannah."

"Why's that, exactly?"

Brody stilled, and then realized what was happening. Reece had been friends with Hannah long before he met Brody. He and Reece were close, but Brody had a feeling that his friend was not too happy with him for putting Hannah in this position. There was only one thing to say, and that was the truth.

"Because I love her."

"Yeah?"

"Yeah."

"She's a good person, Brody. I had my doubts before I saw the two of you together, but if you don't mean it, then let her go now. She's not as used to this kind of thing. Let her walk away."

"I can't let her walk away, Reece. Not again. She's

the one. I never believed there was such a thing, one person you could imagine spending every day and every night with, but I do now. I believe it. I need to make her believe it."

Reece nodded and waved him in. "Okay, then. Back to the ranch?"

"I need to go by my parents' place first, to get something from my mom."

"What?"

"My grandmother's ring."

Reece's expression broke into a full smile, and he nodded approvingly. "Now, that's more like it. Do you think your mom will make me some of her fried chicken?"

Brody rolled his eyes, letting his head fall back against the seat. All he could think about was getting that ring and convincing Hannah to give him one more shot. A real shot.

"I have to warn you, she'll like me even more now that I'm going to be a dad." Reece said the words so casually that Brody didn't even register them for several seconds.

"Did you just say—"

"I did. Abby called me in France to let me know. We didn't plan on it, but it was a great surprise. It's still a little strange to say it out loud."

Brody slapped Reece on the shoulder, and then shook his hand.

"Congratulations, man. You guys are going to be the best parents."

Brody suddenly pictured Hannah, at some point in the future, telling him she was pregnant—with his baby. The thought left him reeling.

He had to make this work.

Luckily, a while later, as he explained everything, his parents agreed. They liked Hannah, and they were as outraged as he was when he filled them in on what had happened.

"I thought you'd be upset that I lied to you about the retirement, and the thing with Hannah," he said to his mom, feeling about twelve years old again, fighting the urge to scrape his shoe on the kitchen floor.

"Honey, we knew something was up all along. You just weren't yourself since you came home. But we figured you'd tell us in your own time. Until Hannah showed up, and then we saw your spark come back. When you told me that silly story about her not wanting a ring, we knew that was strange, too, but we trusted you'd work it out on your own. But that picture…that poor girl," his mom said with a sigh.

Reece looked on, munching on some of the leftover fried chicken.

"You had better have a good plan to make it up to her, Brody. She didn't deserve that," his father said sternly.

He looked at the ring in his hand, opening the old velvet box.

"I plan to, Dad. If she'll let me."

"That ring was your grandmother's, and she wore it for the fifty-seven years of her marriage. She said it was yours when you found the right woman, and frankly, we never thought you'd get to put it on anyone's finger. We hope it brings you the same happiness it brought your grandparents."

Brody's eyes stung a little, to his chagrin, as he

looked at the pristine, antique Tiffany diamond surrounded by sapphires.

"Me, too," he said, clearing his throat and turning to Reece. "Ready?"

"Let's go."

As Reece drove, Brody's mind was spinning as he rehearsed all of the things he wanted to say to Hannah. His hands were cold with nerves as they pulled up to the ranch, but it appeared that he was nervous for no reason.

Her car was gone.

Getting out of the Ferrari and running into the house ahead of Reece, he found Abby sitting at the table, looking worried.

"Where's Hannah?" Brody asked, his heart slamming.

Abby shook her head. "I don't know. I'm sorry, Brody. I might have pressured her to come out with me today, to shake some of this off. I went back to our room to get some things, and then I found a note here telling me she was sorry for letting everyone down, but she had to get away and think. That was two hours ago."

Abby's eyes filled, and Reece crossed the room quickly to pull her up against him. His friend's face was such a study in love and concern that Brody ached as he watched them.

That was what he wanted with Hannah. What he should have given her instead of lies and temporary proposals. The shame he felt was deep and sharp. He had a lot of making up to do, to everyone.

"You don't have anything to be sorry for, Abby. Believe me, that's all me," he said before he ran upstairs, throwing open the door to his room. He let out the breath he was holding as he saw her bags were in the room. That meant she hadn't left for good. There was still a chance.

Back downstairs, he grabbed his keys and headed for the door.

"Where are you going?"

He met Reece's and Abby's concerned gazes.

"To find her, and to make things right, if I can."

14

HANNAH PULLED UP to the house hours after dark, not sure if she was relieved or not to see that Brody's car wasn't there. Had he not come home at all? She shifted uncomfortably in the seat, reminded of when she'd arrived, almost two weeks ago. He had wanted her to leave, but she wouldn't, so he had left instead. She'd waited him out.

Maybe he was waiting her out this time. Waiting for her to leave.

Lights were still on in the house, and the Ferrari was out front, so Reece and Abby were there. She hated worrying her friends. She approached the porch, walking inside to find the couple curled up together on the front room sofa, watching TV. Abby was snoozing on Reece's lap, and Reece was dozing off, too, but they both sat up when she entered.

"Hannah, oh, thank goodness. Are you okay? Where have you been? Did Brody find you? Is he here?" Abby's questions were quick and anxious.

"I was out driving around, thinking. I'm sorry, you

guys, again. I didn't mean to worry anyone. So Brody's not here? I noticed his car was gone."

"No. He went looking for you hours ago."

Hannah covered her face with her hands. "Oh, no. We must have been out there circling around each other all day. I hope he's okay."

"Give him a call, Hannah. You guys need to talk."

She nodded and thanked them both, heading back out to the porch. There, she called Brody's number with slightly trembling fingers, only to have it go to message.

"Hi, um…I'm back at the ranch. I'll wait for you. Call if you can to let me know you're okay, all right?"

She hung up and stood, aimless, wondering what to do now. No way could she sleep, even if she was exhausted.

She headed toward the barns, restless and not wanting to go back inside. She also wanted to see the horses one last time. She'd miss Zip, especially, after she left.

Tears threatened again, but she blinked them back. No more of that.

Inside the barn, she flicked on the light by the door, just one, so that she didn't get the animals too excited. Zip was the only one awake; it figured. The others slumbered easily in the straw beds of their stalls.

Pepper was standing up, but the easy drape of his head over the door of the stall and his shuttered eyes signaled that he was asleep. The others rested easily on their sides or against the inside walls, feeling safe in their environment while trusty Zip was on the lookout.

"Hey Zip," Hannah crooned, linking her arms

around his neck and laying her cheek on his smooth, muscular neck. She smiled when he nickered reassuringly, giving her his familiar nudge.

"I'm going to have to leave soon, but I want you to be good. No throwing people, especially Brody, okay?"

Zip apparently didn't agree with that, swinging his head to the other side of the door, leaving her hanging.

"I don't think he likes that idea any more than I do."

Hannah spun to find Brody standing in the doorway under the light. He looked as if he'd had as hard a day as she had.

"I left you a message. Just a few minutes ago."

It was as far as Hannah got; she had no idea what to say.

"I got it. I hoped you wouldn't take off before I got back. I guess I couldn't blame you if you had," he said. "But I'm glad you didn't."

"I had to get away and think. Abby… She wanted me to chin up and go out with her this afternoon, but I couldn't. It was a lousy thing to do, I know, ditching her, but I was so…confused. And angry. I couldn't take facing people."

"She was worried about you, but she understood. She knew she'd pushed too hard."

"I'll talk to her. I shouldn't have upset her in her, um—" Hannah stopped, not knowing whether she should share Abby's news.

"In her condition?" Brody filled in the blank, smiling slightly.

"You know?"

"Yeah, Reece told me. You'd think he won the lottery. I guess he has."

"Yeah. I'm happy for them, though I feel terrible, especially after everything they did for us. They're so understanding. It makes me feel even worse."

"They're good friends."

Hannah nodded, unsure what to say next. They'd talked about everything but each other and the problems at hand for long enough.

"Where did you go?" she asked.

He stepped farther inside. "To the track. Driving helps me focus, clear out the clutter. You?"

"I ended up over at that spot that overlooks the wetlands."

He nodded, knowing exactly where she meant.

"Are you okay?" he asked.

Hannah hesitated. "I guess so. Maybe I'm just worn out."

"Me, too. But I'm glad that you're back. I hope you didn't mean what you were saying to Zip. Why do you want to leave?"

She shrugged. "I figured you'd want me to now. But also…I think I should."

He closed the space between them quickly, his expression intense, ragged with raw emotion as he held her shoulders in his hands, regarding her with such ferocity she nearly stepped back.

"Why would you think I want you to leave? That's the last thing I want."

"Because all of this is my doing, really. I never should have told that reporter I was your fiancée, and I never should have done what I did in the gazebo or—"

"What happened in the gazebo was one of the best

moments in my life," he said. Then, as if needing to emphasize the point, Brody kissed her, long and hard.

When he pulled back, they were both breathing unevenly. "Don't you dare regret that. Or any of it. None of this was your fault, Hannah. Not a single thing. I never should have played their stupid games from the start, let alone brought you into it. You were a friend, wanting a new start in life, and I…should have known better."

Hannah sighed, putting her hand to one side of his face, her heart aching as he rubbed a scruffy cheek on her palm.

She loved him so much it hurt.

"Well, I guess we can agree that we both made some bad decisions, then, but it's my own fault I let myself get so far off course. And that's what I was thinking about today. How do I get back on track? I thought I had found my direction, but—"

"What do you mean? Your pictures, your articles—"

"They all fell through—two publications decided I wasn't credible enough, I guess, and the other one, um…the editor told me you contacted him, asked for a favor. Somehow his boss suddenly thinks my work isn't quite right for them."

Brody stilled. "I'm so sorry, Hannah. I wanted to help if I could. You were doing so much for me. Giving so much up. I thought— It was just a phone call. But I should have asked you."

"I know. I was angry at first, but I know you meant well. And it made me realize that I'd lost sight of my own goals. It all happened too fast, too easily and that's why it fell apart so quickly, too. I didn't really earn that success, it just happened. Largely because of you. That was the only reason they wanted me at all."

"No. I don't believe that. Your photos and ideas are great."

"Apparently not that great, but that's okay. I can get better, which is what I intend to do."

Brody said nothing, but paced in frustration, running his hands through his hair as he often did. It left him looking ruffled and wilder than usual. Hannah's gaze devoured him greedily, as if she needed enough to last her for a very long time.

"What does that mean?" he asked, looking wary.

She pulled her shoulders straight, standing tall. "It means I have to figure it out. I have to get back on the road and find the stories I was meant to tell. Start again. Make my own success, build it up so that it's really mine and won't blow apart at the first hard break."

She swallowed hard, making herself not look away from him. She owed him that. "I have to go, Brody. I have to get back to my life and let you get back to yours, especially after I ruined everything for you. I'm so sorry."

"You did nothing of the sort, Hannah. You…made it all worthwhile."

"I know you're trying to be kind, but—"

Brody stopped pacing and uttered a harsh chuckle. "Well, you see, that's where you're wrong. For all the lies and fakery, the person I was lying to the most was myself, and you, I suppose. But I'm not lying now, Hannah. You have to believe that."

"I don't understand, what—"

"I love you. I love you down to the bottom of my soul, and I knew it all the time. I knew a while ago that I wanted you to stay and that I wanted to marry you and not have it end in a few months, or ever. I knew I wanted to sit at that table in our room every morning and have coffee before we go down to take care of the horses. But I was too chicken to say so. I was too caught up in my past, in reliving what I was before to think of being someone new. I thought… Actually, I don't know what I thought. All I do know is that I don't want you to leave."

Hannah was in shock, hardly believing what she was hearing.

Brody stepped up close to her again.

"Please, Hannah, don't go. I love you. I get what you're saying. I need to find a new path, too. We could do that together. You asked me to show you how to take chances, but really, I need you to show me that. How to move forward…how to build a new life."

She wanted it to be real, to be true, but it was hard to tell anymore.

"Brody, I love you, too, but—"

"Say it again," he demanded, pressing in, his body hot against hers.

"I love you," she said tenderly, looking up into his face. "Right down to the bottom of my soul as well, but—"

"Say it again," he whispered against her mouth.

Hannah caught her breath, her thoughts muddling, her focus blurring.

"I love you, but I—"

He kissed her then, and really made her lose track of what she was trying to tell him, pressing her flush against the stable door, letting her feel how much he wanted her.

How much he loved her.

It was in the tenderness of the kiss, how his hands cradled her head and how he wouldn't let her finish telling him why she had to go.

Right now, she wasn't too sure herself.

"I love you, Hannah," he said again, too. "No buts about it."

Hannah truly didn't know what to say. She'd thought she'd figured it out, but that was when she'd assumed he'd want her to go. Now he clearly didn't.

He thought she was brave? That she was the one who could help him move forward?

"I worry that when the smoke clears and it's back to everyday life, you'll resent that I ruined this for you," she said, since they were being honest. She knew that if she stayed and he ended up not wanting her, it would destroy her.

His lips were on her neck now. "That's never going to happen. If I want to go back to racing, I will. None of that is your fault, but…"

"What?" she asked breathlessly.

"I was suffering from tunnel vision before, so I couldn't see it, but I've enjoyed my time with the young guys, helping them out. I was talking to Reece about it. I love driving, but I also love teaching those kids to drive and keeping them off the streets. Reece suggested starting a real school, and it felt right. But I need to consider it more seriously. We can figure all that out together, though, right?"

Hannah moaned and curled her fingers into his shirt as he honed in on a particularly sensitive cluster of nerve endings and, sensing her response, stayed there for a while.

Until a large, heavy horse head nudged them both aside.

Hannah couldn't help but laugh.

"I guess Zip has had enough of this."

Brody gave the horse a withering look. Zip just snorted.

"He's going to have to put up with it for a few more minutes."

Hannah followed as Brody pulled her forward, away from the stall into the light near the doorway. Taking a deep breath, he pulled something from his pocket. Then, to her shock, he bent down on one knee, her hand in his.

Hannah froze, watching as he opened the small velvet box, the contents shining up at her like a promise.

"Hannah, I love you. I know this might not be the best time, but whatever you decide to do, I hope you'll decide to do it with me. This ring was my grandmother's, and I want it to be yours. Please don't leave."

"Brody, I—"

"Marry me, Hannah. For real. Forever."

Hannah opened her mouth to answer, but he stopped her again. Instead of slipping the ring on her finger, he put the box in her palm, closing her fingers over it.

"The wedding is tomorrow afternoon. I'll be there, and I'll have the rings. I'm going to stay at my folks' house, so you can have some time and space to think, some room to decide. I want you to be as sure as I am. No more being impulsive and jumping in. And if you decide not, and that you have to go, then I respect that, too, but maybe someday…"

Hannah opened her hand and stared at the box, her mind officially blown. If this day threw any more surprises at her, she wasn't sure if she could handle it all.

He stood and kissed her one more time before he turned away, leaving the barn, heading back up to his car.

To leave her to think. But Hannah didn't need to think, analyze or reconsider. She knew what she wanted as surely as she knew her own name. It wasn't impulsive or a leap of faith because it was what she'd wanted all along.

She took off after Brody, chasing him up the hill. He had reached the Charger and was opening the door.

"Brody," she called, stopping him. "Wait."

Hannah was out of breath by the time she caught up and took his hand, putting the box back in his hand.

He pulled back, straightening, his expression solemn. He nodded.

"Okay, I understand."

"No, you don't. You had it almost right, but in my fantasy proposal, the one I told you about before, you don't hand a girl a box, you put the ring on her finger."

He seemed stunned, his eyes widening as he fell to his knee again, not taking his eyes off her. The box bounced to the pavement, the ring in his hand as he took her left one in his.

"Hannah, are you sure you don't need time to decide? I want you to be sure. I know you want to be unpredictable and adventurous, but this time, I want you to be as sure as I am."

"Brody," she said with a smile, "I've never been

as sure of anything in my life. Put the ring on, would you?"

He did, and Hannah felt her chest tighten when she saw his hand tremble slightly.

"We don't have to get married tomorrow. We can be engaged for as long as you want," he said.

When the ring was on, she gripped his hand in hers.

"No, let's do it. I mean, everyone is here and we already have the ceremony planned, right? I have a feeling we'll have plenty of adventure ahead of us, and I still intend to pursue photojournalism, maybe traveling to the far ends of the globe, who knows? But being with you is my greatest adventure. So why not go for it?"

She was smiling and crying, and Brody laughed, a full, loud laugh. It brought Reece and Abby out onto the porch, Hannah realized, hearing the door slam as Brody picked her up and spun her around.

He set her down and kissed her as Reece and Abby hooted and hollered in approval. Their friends came over to congratulate them, and when Brody looked at her, it was with all the love she could imagine in his eyes.

"This is going to be fun," he said with a big, Brody-style grin.

Hannah didn't doubt it for a second.

"Wow." AIDEN BREATHED out the word as he stood with Brody, taking in the lineup of stock cars on the street outside his parents' condo. "This is awesome."

"It certainly is," Brody agreed, feeling a depth of gratitude he couldn't quite express.

"I think you might find yourself driving one some-day," Brody said to his nephew.

"More likely building them, I think," Aiden re-sponded.

"What?"

Aiden shrugged. "Ever since you've been teaching us so much about the cars, and working with me on the Mustang, I really like learning about how the en-gines work. I've been doing a lot of reading. Maybe Mom is right. I could go to college, get an engineering degree and design race cars, make them even better. I still get to drive them anyway."

Brody laughed. "Of course. That's a terrific idea, Aiden." He was moved to have had that influence on his nephew. "Where is your mom?"

"Inside—she was running around, saying some-thing about getting all the flowers right at the last minute and how you can never make up your mind."

"Ah."

The racing community, his friends, his team… everyone, really, had come out in support of him and Hannah. It was more than he'd hoped for.

Hannah had blogged about their wedding that morning, and his fans had approved, as well. It turned out they liked Wild Brody Palmer as he was, and they loved his wild bride, too.

They wanted him back in racing as well, but Brody wasn't going to rush in. Racing life would mean months away from home, and as he helped Hannah out of the Charger, he thought he might have better things to do with his time.

"You look incredible," he said, taking in her shimmering, sleeveless white dress. Simple, but so incredibly sexy.

"Thank you. You should wear suits more often," she said warmly, pushing up on the toes of her sandals to kiss his cheek.

"I'll consider it."

"I have a surprise for you, too," she said, her cheeks pink.

The perfect combination of sexy and sultry. That was his Hannah.

"What's that?"

"Well, you weren't supposed to see until later, but…" She winked, putting her foot on the curb and lifting up the edge of her dress to reveal a garter with his racing number on it.

"We're never going to make it through the reception," Brody said, staring hungrily at her thigh and loving the garter that was sure to be his favorite piece of racing memorabilia ever.

She laughed and held out her hand. "Want to go get married? Forever, this time?"

"Absolutely."

Hand in hand, surrounded by family and friends, Hannah and Brody walked to the beach, all of their adventures ahead of them.

* * * * *

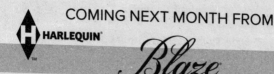
#835 SEARCH AND SEDUCE
Uniformly Hot!
by Sara Jane Stone

This time, Amy Benton is writing the rules: no strings, no promises and definitely no soldiers. Once she sees gorgeous pararescue jumper Mark Rhodes shirtless, though, she just may break every one...

#836 UNDER THE SURFACE
SEALs of Fortune
by Kira Sinclair

Former SEAL Jackson Duchane is searching for a sunken ship full of gold. Business rival Loralei Lancaster is determined to beat him to it. The race is on—if they can stay out of bed long enough to find the treasure.

#837 ANYWHERE WITH YOU
Made in Montana
by Debbi Rawlins

Stuntman and all-around bad boy Ben Wolf is only visiting Blackfoot Falls for a few days. But Deputy Grace Hendrix makes him want to get in trouble with the law...in a whole new way!

#838 PULLED UNDER
Pleasure Before Business
by Kelli Ireland

When Harper Banks barged into his club, Levi Walsh was ready to dress her down...all the way to her lacy lingerie. Until she tells him she's an IRS investigator—and she's closing his business!

REQUEST YOUR FREE BOOKS!
2 FREE NOVELS PLUS 2 FREE GIFTS!

HARLEQUIN®

Blaze®

red-hot reads!

YES! Please send me 2 FREE Harlequin® Blaze™ novels and my 2 FREE gifts (gifts are worth about $10). After receiving them, if I don't wish to receive any more books, I can return the shipping statement marked "cancel." If I don't cancel, I will receive 4 brand-new novels every month and be billed just $4.74 per book in the U.S. or $4.96 per book in Canada. That's a savings of at least 14% off the cover price. It's quite a bargain. Shipping and handling is just 50¢ per book in the U.S. and 75¢ per book in Canada.* I understand that accepting the 2 free books and gifts places me under no obligation to buy anything. I can always return a shipment and cancel at any time. Even if I never buy another book, the two free books and gifts are mine to keep forever.

150/350 HDN F4WC

Name	(PLEASE PRINT)
Address	Apt. #
City	State/Prov.	Zip/Postal Code

Signature (if under 18, a parent or guardian must sign)

Mail to the Harlequin® Reader Service:
IN U.S.A.: P.O. Box 1867, Buffalo, NY 14240-1867
IN CANADA: P.O. Box 609, Fort Erie, Ontario L2A 5X3

Want to try two free books from another line?
Call 1-800-873-8635 or visit www.ReaderService.com.

* Terms and prices subject to change without notice. Prices do not include applicable taxes. Sales tax applicable in N.Y. Canadian residents will be charged applicable taxes. Offer not valid in Quebec. This offer is limited to one order per household. Not valid for current subscribers to Harlequin Blaze books. All orders subject to credit approval. Credit or debit balances in a customer's account(s) may be offset by any other outstanding balance owed by or to the customer. Please allow 4 to 6 weeks for delivery. Offer available while quantities last.

Your Privacy—The Harlequin® Reader Service is committed to protecting your privacy. Our Privacy Policy is available online at www.ReaderService.com or upon request from the Harlequin Reader Service.

We make a portion of our mailing list available to reputable third parties that offer products we believe may interest you. If you prefer that we not exchange your name with third parties, or if you wish to clarify or modify your communication preferences, please visit us at www.ReaderService.com/consumerchoice or write to us at Harlequin Reader Service Preference Service, P.O. Box 9062, Buffalo, NY 14269. Include your complete name and address.

HB13R2

Mark had been her husband's best friend. Was it wrong to want more from him than a shoulder to cry on?

Read on for a sneak preview of
SEARCH AND SEDUCE,
*a **UNIFORMLY HOT!** novel*
by Sara Jane Stone.

"In those first few months, I made a cup of cocoa every night. Then I'd sit here and email you."

"You stopped sending memories of Darren," Mark said. "About six months ago."

"You noticed." Amy lowered the mug, a line of hot chocolate on her upper lip.

His gaze locked on her mouth. He wanted to lean forward and kiss her lips clean.

She shrugged. "I guess I was done living in the past. It was a good idea, though. It helped me find my way through it all."

He stared at their joined hands. "Must have been, if you started a new list."

Her fingers pressed against his skin. "This one's different."

"I know." He felt her drawing closer.

"I'm writing the rules this time." Her eyes lit with excitement. Unable to look away, Mark saw the moment desire rose up to meet her newfound joy.

He withdrew his hand. "I should go."

Mark pushed back from the table and stood. But Amy followed, stepping close, invading his space. Her hands rose, and before he could move away, he felt her palms touch his face.

He froze, not daring to move. He didn't even blink, just stared down at her. Her gaze narrowed in on his lips, her body shifting closer. Rising on to her tiptoes, she touched her lips to his.

Mark closed his eyes, his hands forming tight fists at his sides. He felt her tongue touch his lower lip as if asking for more. Unable to hold back, he gave in, opening his mouth to her kiss, deepening it, making it clear that this kiss was not tied to an offering of friendship and comfort.

Amy's hands moved over his jaw, running up through his hair. Pulling his mouth tightly against hers. He groaned. She tasted like chocolate—sweet and delicious. He wanted more, so damn much more.

Her fingers ran down the front of his shirt, moving lower and lower. His body hardened, ready and wanting.

He reached for her wrist, gently drawing her away. Then he leaned closer, his lips touching her ear, allowing her to hear the low growl of need in his voice. "Let me know when you've written your rules."

Don't miss
SEARCH AND SEDUCE by Sara Jane Stone,
available March 2015 wherever
Harlequin® Blaze® books and ebooks are sold.

www.Harlequin.com

JUST CAN'T GET ENOUGH?

Join our social communities
and talk to us online.

You will have access to the latest
news on upcoming titles and special
promotions, but most importantly,
you can talk to other fans about your
favorite Harlequin reads.

Harlequin.com/Community

Facebook.com/HarlequinBooks

Twitter.com/HarlequinBooks

Pinterest.com/HarlequinBooks

JUST CAN'T GET ENOUGH
ROMANCE
Looking for more?

Harlequin has everything from contemporary, passionate and heartwarming to suspenseful and inspirational stories.

Whatever your mood, we have a romance just for you!

Connect with us to find your next great read, special offers and more.

Facebook.com/HarlequinBooks

Twitter.com/HarlequinBooks

HarlequinBlog.com

Harlequin.com/Newsletters

www.Harlequin.com